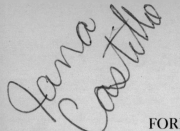

FOREVER ENEMIES

Mom read the newspaper headline and article out loud: "*TWO SIXTH-GRADERS FIND BABY GIRL ABANDONED ON SCHOOL STEPS.*

"*Authorities are searching for the parents of a five-month-old baby girl found abandoned on the front steps of Mark Twain Elementary School this morning. A hand-written note pinned to her blanket identified her only as Ashley.*

"*Sixth-grade students Taffy Sinclair and Jana Morgan were walking in the hallway when Miss Sinclair spotted the basket containing the baby outside the glass doors and brought the child inside to the principal's office . . .*"

"MISS SINCLAIR!" I shrieked. "What about me? I'm the one who heard Ashley crying! I'm just as important as Taffy! She wouldn't even have looked out the front door if I hadn't made her stop and listen."

I couldn't believe it. Taffy must have said something to the reporter to make him think that she found Ashley practically single-handedly. I had been stupid to think anything was different between us. She hadn't changed. She was still just as much my enemy as ever. . . .

TAFFY SINCLAIR, BABY ASHLEY, AND ME

Betsy Haynes

A BANTAM SKYLARK BOOK®
TORONTO · NEW YORK · LONDON · SYDNEY · AUCKLAND

RL 5, 009–12

TAFFY SINCLAIR, BABY ASHLEY, AND ME

A Bantam Skylark Book / January 1988
3 printings through September 1988

Skylark Books is a registered trademark of Bantam Books,
a division of Bantam Doubleday Dell Publishing Group, Inc.
Registered in U.S. Patent and Trademark Office and elsewhere.

ISBN 0-553-15713-2

Published simultaneously in the United States and Canada

Bantam Books are published by Bantam Books, a division of Bantam
Doubleday Dell Publishing Group, Inc. Its trademark, consisting of the
words "Bantam Books" and the portrayal of a rooster, is Registered
in U.S. Patent and Trademark Office and in other countries. Marca
Registrada. Bantam Books, 666 Fifth Avenue, New York, New York 10103.

PRINTED IN THE UNITED STATES OF AMERICA

S   11 10 9 8 7 6 5 4 3

For Joan Vincenti Cairatti

1 ✻

"Oh, Jana. How darling. That must be the very latest hairstyle."

Little explosions started going off in my brain, and I whirled around to face Taffy Sinclair. It was almost time for the first bell, and she was standing beside her locker with an icky sweet smile on her face. Mona Vaughn was with her and so was Alexis Duvall. I thought I'd die.

"Of course it's the lastest style," I snapped. "Haven't you noticed it in all the magazines?"

I hugged my books to my chest and stomped on past Taffy, trying to tune out the snickers that followed me down the hall. *Of course* Taffy Sinclair would notice my hair. And *of course* she would make a big deal out of it in front of everybody. Taffy Sinclair is my enemy. She may be gorgeous with her long blond hair and big blue eyes, but she is also the snottiest and most stuck-up girl in the sixth grade at Mark Twain Elementary. I'm not the only one who thinks so, but I'm the one she hates most. In fact, she hates me so much that once she even blackmailed me when I found our teacher's wallet after someone else had stolen it.

Anyway, I was so busy getting away from Taffy Sinclair and thinking about what a terrible person she is that I almost had a head-on collision with my best friend, Beth Barry, right in the middle of the hall.

"Hey, slow down, Morgan," Beth said as we stopped a couple of inches apart. "Are you running from a fire?" She looked at me, got a quizzical expression on her face, then added, "What happened to your hair?"

"I forgot to spit out my gum when I went to bed last night, okay?" I grumbled.

"Oh, I get it," Beth said, trying not to laugh. "And it got stuck in your hair right above your left ear, and you had to use scissors to get it out. Right?"

"So?" I said, giving her a blazing look. "SOME people might be polite enough not to point out to their best friend that she has a gigantic hole in her hair right by her face when she obviously already knows it!"

I brushed on past Beth and ducked into the girls' bathroom to check my hair one more time before I went to class. Normally my dark brown hair hid both of my ears and fell all the way to my shoulders, but now all that remained on the left side was a row of fringe, and my ear was sticking straight out like a sail for the whole world to see. If only there were some way I could keep Randy Kirwan from noticing it. Randy is the most wonderful boy in the world, not to mention the handsomest, kindest, and most sensitive boy in my class. He is also my boyfriend, and I always try to look my best for him. But what could I do? For the millionth time, I tried pulling an uncut strand forward to cover my ear, but as soon as I let go of the hair, it fell back into its regular place. I sighed and made a face at myself in the mirror. I looked awful. In fact, I wouldn't look any worse if I had used those scissors to cut off my nose.

I couldn't help feeling miserable. Everything in my life was going wrong. This was the most terrible morning I had ever lived through. First I had dropped my toothbrush into the toilet and had to brush my teeth with my finger. Then I looked into the mirror and saw a big glob of pink bubble gum stuck in my hair. And finally, to top it off, Mom hadn't even noticed my hair. She had been too preoccupied. When I came into the kitchen for breakfast, she had a dreamy look on her face and then made the big announcement that she had finally decided to marry her boyfriend, Pink.

How could she do that to me? After all the times she had said that she didn't want to rush into marriage again. But I didn't have time to think about that right now. The first bell was ringing and I had to get to class.

Even though I made it to the classroom before the second bell, I was the last person in the room. My four best friends were already in their seats, and so was Taffy Sinclair. Wiggins was writing the math assignment on the board with her back to the class. I had to go by Taffy's desk to get to mine, and I stuck my nose in the air, raised my left hand to cover my ear, and started to march right past. I wasn't going to give her the chance to make fun of my hair again. Just then I stumbled, tripping over something in the aisle. My books went flying as I caught myself.

"Taffy Sinclair!" I shrieked. "You tripped me! Miss Wiggins, Taffy Sinclair stuck her foot out when I went by and tripped me."

Taffy came up out of her seat like an erupting volcano. "Liar!" she screamed. "I didn't trip you. You're probably so clumsy that you fell over your own feet."

"I did not! You tripped me!"

"YOUNG LADIES!" Wiggins turned around so abruptly that her red curls were bouncing, and she had on her I've-had-it frown. "Will you please get control of yourselves?" She paused and the room went deadly silent. "Now, what seems to be the problem? Jana, you may begin."

"She tripped me, Miss Wiggins. Honest, she did. I was just walking to my seat minding my own business."

"I did not," Taffy blurted. I could see that she was trying to squeeze fake tears out of her eyes. "She tripped herself, and now she's trying to get ME into trouble."

Wiggins didn't say anything for a minute, and I could practically hear the computer in her brain clicking away, comparing our arguments. I held my breath. She would probably believe Taffy Sinclair instead of me. Prissy, icky sweet Taffy, who always buttered up the teachers. Besides, why should Wiggins care if I was having a horrible day, and my toothbrush fell into the toilet, and I had to cut a huge glob of bubble gum out of my hair, and my mother was going to marry Wallace Pinkerton, and Taffy Sinclair had stuck out her foot and tripped me? Why should *she* care about any of it? It wasn't her problem.

Wiggins cleared her throat. "Jana and Taffy," she began, frowning at us over the top of her wire-frame glasses. "I think that what we need here is a cooling-off period before we discuss this situation any further. I will give each of you a hall pass, and I want you to take your math books and this morning's assignment and spend the rest of the period in the detention room in the principal's office. Perhaps the two of you will be ready for civilized discussion after that."

My heart sank. I had never been sent to the detention room in my life. Mostly only rowdy kids like Clarence Marshall got sent there.

"This is all your fault, Taffy," I snarled as we headed down the hall toward the principal's office a few minutes later. "If you hadn't tripped me, this would never have happened."

Taffy stopped and glared at me. "I did not trip you, Jana Morgan. Don't blame me if you're so graceful that you fell over your own feet."

I hated Taffy Sinclair more than I had ever hated her before. I wanted to punch her out, but I knew I would only get into more trouble than I was already in, so I shot her a poison-dart look and stormed on down the hall as fast as I could with her charging along right behind me. She probably didn't want me to get there first and tell my side of the story to Mrs. Winchell, the principal.

Just as we started to go past the glass double front doors, I stopped. I thought I had heard a sound. Taffy stopped, too, and looked at me.

"What's the matter?" she demanded.

"I heard a noise," I snapped. "A kitten or something."

"What? A kitten in the school?"

"*Shhh!* Listen!"

The sound came again, and this time Taffy heard it, too. "It *does* sound like a kitten. I wonder how it got into the building."

We both looked up and down the silent hallway. I couldn't see the kitten or anything else that looked as if it could be making that sound.

"Maybe it got trapped in one of the lockers," I suggested.

Taffy nodded, and we each took one side of the hall and walked along next to the lockers, listening carefully. When we reached the end of them, we turned around and came back again, still listening. Nothing. Then I scanned the tops of the lockers in case it had climbed up there and couldn't get down. Nope. There was no kitten stranded up there, either.

I shrugged and continued on toward the principal's office when suddenly Taffy gasped and raced to the glass front doors, pushing them open and slipping outside. I turned to look at her and saw her shivering in the cold autumn wind and bending over a basket on the front steps of the school. It was a small basket, filled with what looked like an old, faded blanket.

In an instant Taffy scooped up the basket and scrambled back inside. "It's a . . . a baby!" she sputtered.

It *was* a baby wrapped up in blankets and lying in the basket. Its eyes were closed and its face was screwed into a pitiful expression as it made the high-pitched little cries that I had mistaken for the sound of a kitten.

"Oh, my gosh." I tiptoed closer and stared at the bundle in Taffy's arms. My heart was hammering away. I couldn't believe it. We had found a real live baby! It was like something in a dream!

Just then I noticed that there was a wrinkled scrap of paper pinned to the blanket with words written on it in pencil. "It's a note!" I cried, and reached out to smooth the paper so that we both could read it.

MY NAME IS ASHLEY. PLEASE TAKE GOOD CARE OF ME.

"Ashley," I whispered.

At the sound of her name, Ashley opened her eyes. Then she stopped crying and started to smile. I leaned forward and wrapped my arms around the basket, too. Taffy and I just stood there in the silent hallway, holding the baby between us and staring down at her beautiful face. Then we slowly raised our eyes until we were looking at each other. Neither of us could say a word.

2 ✤

"Let's put the basket down and look at her to make sure she's okay." Taffy's eyes were bright with excitement.

I nodded, still unable to speak around the lump in my throat. Ashley was the most beautiful baby I had ever seen. She had reddish-gold hair that curled into soft ringlets around her face and eyes as blue as the sky.

I could hear the muffled voice of a teacher coming from a classroom somewhere down the long hallway and the clackety-clack of a typewriter in the office, but they seemed a million miles away as we carefully placed the basket on the floor between us and knelt beside it in the empty hallway.

Ashley was still smiling, and now she was waving a tiny fist in the air as if she wanted to hold hands. I giggled and offered her my finger, which she grabbed and held onto with surprising strength.

Very gently Taffy pulled the blanket away. The baby was wearing a pink terry cloth sleeper with a bunny on the front. It was clean but faded, and one of Ashley's tiny toes poked out through a hole in the foot.

"She looks okay." I slowly exhaled a deep breath that I didn't realize I had been holding.

"Yeah." Taffy grinned broadly. "She looks super."

I bent forward and sniffed a couple of times. "She smells okay, too."

We both giggled at that, then Taffy said, "She really likes us. Look at her grin."

Taffy was right. Ashley hadn't cried once since she saw us, and now she was gurgling happily and drooling bubbles as she concentrated on drawing my finger toward her mouth.

"Look at her pull on your finger," said Taffy. "Do you think she's hungry?"

"Gosh. I don't know." With my free hand I dug around in the basket until my fingers touched something hard and round. It was a bottle, and when I pulled it out of the basket, I could see that it was full of milk. I pulled the cover off the nipple and held the bottle near her mouth. "Here, little Ashley," I cooed. "Do you want your bottle?"

She let go of my finger at once and began eagerly sucking on the nipple. "Look, Taffy," I said in amazement. "Isn't she wonderful?"

Taffy reached out and stroked her forehead, smiling down at her. "Oh, yes," she said in a breathless whisper.

When Ashley had finished all that she wanted of her bottle, I gently lifted her onto my shoulder and patted her on the back until she got a bubble up. Then I put her back into the basket. She was content now, and she made sweet little cooing sounds and smiled at us.

She was so small and precious, like a real live doll. I wanted to sit there beside her forever, to hold her and play with her, but a warning bell was going off in my brain. We weren't her mothers. We were just a couple of sixth-graders who had found her on the doorstep of the school.

Taffy must have been reading my mind. "What are we going to do now?" she asked softly.

I looked around helplessly until I spotted the sign beside the front door: All Visitors Must Register in the Office.

"We'd better take Ashley into the office and show her to Mrs. Winchell," I said. "She'll know what to do."

"You're right." Taffy jumped to her feet. "I'll put our books in my locker for now."

I felt better. I liked Mrs. Winchell. Besides being the school principal, she is the mother of one of my best friends, Christie. I knew that she was someone we could trust to help us take care of Ashley.

I pulled the blanket up and tucked it in around Ashley while Taffy ran to her locker. When she came back, we lifted the basket so that we could carry it between us and headed for the office. Our footsteps echoed in the empty hall. It seemed like hours ago that we had been going to that very place, and we had been fighting like crazy. I looked out of the corner of my eye at Taffy. She must have been thinking about the very same thing because she was looking at me, too.

With the basket between us we had to turn sideways to get through the office door. We walked up to the counter and waited for someone to notice us. My heart was starting to hammer again. I could hardly wait to tell our story to Mrs. Winchell and see her face when she heard how we had thought at first that the cries were being made by a kitten.

No one noticed us. Mrs. Lockwood, the school secretary, was sitting at her desk behind the counter, totaling lunch money. Mrs. Gray, who teaches after-noon kindergarten, was checking her box in the teachers' mailbox, and Mr. Rollins, the science teacher, was running off study sheets on the copy machine. I shifted my weight from one foot to the other and thought about clearing my throat to get someone's attention. I didn't have to. Ashley picked that instant to start crying again, and she let out such a squall that I almost dropped my side of the basket.

"What was that?" cried Mrs. Lockwood, shooting straight up out of her chair. Then she spotted Taffy and me. "Girls! What's in the basket?" Suddenly her eyes opened wide, registering surprise. "Oh, my word. It's a baby!"

"I found her on the front steps of the school," Taffy began excitedly.

"But it was after *I* heard her crying," I corrected. "She would never have seen the basket if I hadn't heard the baby crying first."

Taffy shot me a poison-dart look. "Only Jana thought it was a kitten. I was the one who noticed the basket through the glass doors and carried her inside."

"Girls. Girls. This is no time to argue. Put the basket up on the counter before you drop it," Mrs. Lockwood ordered. "Mrs. Winchell!" she called over her shoulder. "Somebody get Mrs. Winchell. I think she's on the phone."

Before Taffy and I could even start to lift the basket up onto the counter ourselves, Mr. Rollins reached across and took it out of our arms.

"Poor little thing," he said as he set Ashley on the desk on the other side of the counter where Taffy and I couldn't even see her anymore. "Did somebody leave you on our front doorstep?"

By this time Mrs. Gray had rushed up and was peering into the basket at the crying baby. too. "Hush, hush, little baby," she cooed. Then she bent closer. "Look. There's a note pinned to the blanket."

"It SAYS that her name is ASHLEY," I shouted over the commotion. I was starting to get mad. They had taken our baby away from us, and now they were acting as if we weren't even there. "It says, 'Please take good care of me,'" I said even more loudly. "And that's exactly what Taffy Sinclair and I were doing. Ashley wasn't even crying for us."

"That's right!" Taffy said defiantly. "WE were taking VERY good care of her."

"I'm sure you were, dears," said Mrs. Lockwood. "And thank you for bringing her into the office. But this is a matter for grown-ups to handle now. Go sit down in those chairs against the wall for the time being. Someone will talk to you in a little bit."

I clenched my fists and stomped over to the chairs, sitting down in one of them as hard as I could. Taffy followed me. I could see angry tears welling up in her eyes, and I knew that this time they weren't fake tears.

3 ✳

Just then Mrs. Winchell stepped out of her private office. "Did someone call me? What's going on out here?" At the same instant she spotted Ashley in her basket and rushed forward just as Mrs. Lockwood and the two teachers all started talking at once.

"It's a baby!" cried Mrs. Lockwood in her high-pitched voice. "Someone abandoned her right here, on the front steps of the school."

"She looks okay to me," said Mr. Rollins reassuringly.

"There's a note pinned to the front of her blanket," said Mrs. Gray. "It says her first name is Ashley, but it doesn't say whose baby she is or who left her here."

"Or where she came from," Mrs. Lockwood chimed in.

"We could have told Mrs. Winchell that," I grumbled.

Taffy nodded, and one of her real tears rolled down her cheek. "They don't even care that WE found her," she whispered. "I'll bet they've forgotten that we're even here."

Mrs. Winchell took Ashley out of the basket and cradled her against one shoulder. "She seems to be just fine. But who found her and brought her into the office?" Mrs. Winchell glanced around, spotting Taffy and me for the first time. "Was it you, girls?" she asked in amazement.

"Yes, Mrs. Winchell," I blurted before Mrs. Lockwood could get a word in. "We found her! Out on the front steps! Just a little while ago! Isn't she beautiful?"

"We were on our way to the office, and Jana heard her crying and thought it was a kitten," added Taffy. "Then I looked out the glass doors and saw the basket."

Mrs. Winchell's face lit up. "Goodness. You girls are heroes. Come into my office while I call the police and report this. I'm sure they'll want to thank you, too, and probably ask you a few questions."

Taffy and I stuck our noses into the air and sailed right past the three grown-ups. Ashley peered over Mrs. Winchell's shoulder at us, grinning like a dopey clown. I loved that baby so much I thought my heart was going to burst.

"Relax, girls, and have a seat." Mrs. Winchell smiled kindly at us as she carried Ashley to her desk. "I know this has been a very exciting morning for you."

Taffy and I both nodded and exchanged grins. She could say that again, I thought. It was the most exciting morning of my life. A real, live baby abandoned on the front steps of the school, and Taffy and I had been the ones who found her.

Mrs. Winchell reached for the telephone, and Ashley immediately grabbed the phone cord. "Uh-oh," Mrs. Winchell said with a laugh. "It looks as if I need some help. Here, Taffy, will you hold the baby while I phone the authorities?"

Taffy had reached for Ashley even before Mrs. Winchell stopped speaking. I knew that Taffy was sitting closer to her than I was and that it was easier to hand Ashley to her, but I felt as if someone had just stabbed me in the heart. Taffy had a smug expression on her face as she bounced Ashley on her lap. She's my baby, too! I wanted to shout.

Mrs. Winchell had taken Ashley back again when the police arrived a little while later. There were two officers, a man and a woman, and they smiled politely and introduced themselves when they came into Mrs. Winchell's office.

"Hello, I'm Officer Frost and this is my partner, Officer Martin," the man said.

Mrs. Winchell rose, introduced herself, and then gestured toward Taffy and me. "These are the young ladies who found the baby, Taffy Sinclair and Jana Morgan, and, of course, this is the little girl herself." The officers looked at us and nodded. "The girls behaved very responsibly by bringing her straight to us in the office."

I couldn't help but feel proud, and I could see that both officers were impressed.

Officer Martin opened a notebook and sat on the corner of Mrs. Winchell's desk, facing Taffy and me. "I'll bet it was pretty exciting finding such a cute little baby, wasn't it?" she asked in a friendly voice.

"It sure was," I volunteered. "Her name is Ashley. It's written on a note that is pinned to the front of her blanket."

Officer Martin smiled and wrote something into her notebook, probably Ashley's name. "Okay. Now tell me, which one of you girls actually found Ashley?"

Taffy Sinclair jumped straight out of her chair. "I did!" she said excitedly. "I looked out the glass doors and saw the basket right there on the step."

"But you wouldn't have even looked if I hadn't heard her crying," I interjected. Leave it to Taffy Sinclair to try to take all the credit.

Taffy giggled. "But YOU thought it was a kitten that had accidentally gotten into the school building. You never even thought to look outside."

I started to yell at Taffy that she never would have looked outside if I hadn't made her stop and listen for a kitten, but the officer was talking again.

"So, Taffy, since you were the one who actually went outside and got the basket and brought it inside the building, tell me something. Did you see anyone suspicious near the school? Or anyone running away? Think hard, please. This is important. It could give us the clue we need to find the person who left her here."

Taffy got a stricken look on her face. "I . . . I was only looking at Ashley," she confessed. "I didn't think about looking around."

I knew I was the one with a smug look on my face this time, but I couldn't help it. So Taffy Sinclair had missed something important, huh? That's what she got for being such a show-off. But deep inside I couldn't help wondering if there had been someone hanging around outside, watching. Ashley's mother, maybe. I hadn't thought about Ashley's mother before. She was our baby, and when we found her it had seemed as if she had just been born that very minute. I looked at Taffy. Her face was red and there was another real tear on her cheek.

"I didn't see anyone, either," I offered.

"That's okay, girls," said Officer Martin. "I can understand why you didn't think about looking around. There are other things we can do to try to identify and find her parents."

"Like what?" I couldn't imagine how they could do a thing like that with someone as small as baby Ashley. She couldn't even talk yet.

"We'll check her footprints against the ones the local hospitals keep on file for the babies born there. If that's no help, we'll check the birth certificates, looking for a little girl born around the time she was. Things like that. We're just glad you found her and took such good care of her."

Officer Frost had brought Ashley's basket into Mrs. Winchell's office, and now Officer Martin was taking Ashley from Mrs. Winchell and tucking her inside the blanket.

"What are you going to do?" blurted Taffy.

"We're going to take her down to the station," said Officer Frost.

"And put her in jail?" I cried.

"No, no," he said. "We'll turn her over to our juvenile division, and they'll find a family to take care of her until we find out who she is and where she belongs. She's going to be fine. She's not going to jail."

My heart almost leaped out of my chest. "She could stay at my house," I said. "My mom loves babies. We would take really good care of her. Please?"

"Or my house," said Taffy. "I'd love to keep her at my house, and my mom loves babies, too."

Officer Frost shook his head and smiled kindly. "I'm sure you would both be good mothers to Ashley. You've already demonstrated that. But she will have to go to a regular foster home that has already been approved for cases like this. That's the law."

I fought back tears as I watched the two officers prepare to take Ashley away. They were taking *our baby*. It wasn't fair. We had found her, and we could tell that she loved us as much as we loved her.

"I'm sure arrangements can be made for you girls to visit Ashley," said Officer Martin. "From the way she smiles at you, I'm sure she'll be glad to see you."

"Really?" I said as my spirits soared again. Maybe it wouldn't be so bad after all if they would let us visit her.

Just then there was a knock on the door. We all looked around as a man with a big smile on his face and a camera in his hand stuck his head into the office.

"Hi. Glad I caught you before you took the baby. I'm Herb Little from the *Bridgeport Post*. I just heard about the abandoned baby and the two girls who found her on my police scanner. Mind if I get a picture of the three of them for tonight's paper?"

Taffy and I gasped in unison and looked at each other. Big grins spread across our faces. We were going to have our picture in the paper. Tonight.

"Of course not," said Mrs. Winchell, after she had checked his credentials. "Come on in. And, girls. Let's put your chairs together so that you can hold Ashley between you."

There was a flurry of activity as the photographer got us posed. Ashley smiled through it all, looking up at us as if to say that she was having the time of her life.

We were almost ready when I remembered something critical. "Taffy," I whispered. "Will you do me a huge favor?"

She shrugged. "Sure. What is it?"

"Trade sides with me."

We traded and then smiled while Herb Little took about a jillion shots. Maybe everything was going to work out okay, after all. We would get to visit Ashley, we would have our picture in tonight's *Bridgeport Post*, and because Taffy switched sides with me, nobody would be able to see the huge hole in my hair and my left ear sticking out.

Mr. Little asked us a lot of questions for the article he would write to go with the picture, and, as usual, I had to keep butting in so that Taffy Sinclair didn't take all the credit for finding Ashley. Mrs. Lockwood and the two teachers came into Mrs. Winchell's office and were making cooing noises at Ashley and talking to the police officers and Mr. Little until he left. It was almost like a party for a while. But then, just when things were really getting fun, officers Frost and Martin picked up Ashley, said a quick good-bye, and were gone.

The room got deathly still, and everybody turned and looked at Taffy Sinclair and me, but all I could do was stare at the spot on the desk where Ashley's basket had been sitting until just a moment ago. Suddenly I knew that I was going to cry. I couldn't hold back the tears, and neither could Taffy. Mrs. Lockwood, Mrs. Gray, and Mr. Rollins all looked embarrassed and left the room as fast as they could. I was glad. I don't like it when people see me cry.

"Here, girls," Mrs. Winchell said gently, handing each of us a tissue. "It's perfectly all right to be sad."

Then she left her office, telling us to sit there until we were feeling better.

We didn't talk. We didn't even look at each other. I don't know about Taffy, but I couldn't think about anything but Ashley. Her beautiful smile. Her twinkly eyes. And the way she had pulled on my finger, trying to get it into her mouth. But it had all happened so fast, and now she was gone.

4 ❋

News about our finding an abandoned baby on the front steps traveled around school faster than if it had been gossip. Taffy and I were instant celebrities. And when she heard about Ashley, Wiggins didn't even ask us about the math assignment we were supposed to have done in the detention room. On the playground at recess kids swarmed around us asking questions until we almost couldn't get our breath.

Randy and his friends were shooting baskets and yelling and laughing over by the backboard. I couldn't help noticing that he looked my way several times, and I tried to keep my good side toward him. The one where my hair covered my ear. Once he even missed a rebound because he was looking at me instead of the ball. I smiled to myself and wondered what he was thinking. Did he think that I was a kind and sensitive person for rescuing a tiny, abandoned baby? I certainly hoped so. That would prove to him how much we have in common since he is the most kind and sensitive person I know.

Finally, Beth Barry grabbed me by my coat sleeve and dragged me away from the crowd. Beth is one of my four best friends. The other three are Christie Winchell, Katie Shannon, and Melanie Edwards. We are such good friends that we have a self-improvement club called The Fabulous Five. In the beginning we formed the club to be against Taffy Sinclair. Now we have weekly meetings to try to find ways to become the most gorgeous and most popular girls in Mark Twain Elementary. We even saved our club dues and had blue T-shirts made that say The Fabulous Five across the front in white letters, and we wear them to our meetings.

"Come on, Jana. Tell us exactly what happened," Beth said as she pulled me toward a spot by the fence where The Fabulous Five usually congregates when we want to talk about something private. My other friends were standing there, waiting impatiently to hear my story.

It had to be at least the millionth time I had told it, but I went through the whole thing again about how I had thought I heard a kitten crying and then Taffy looked out the glass doors and saw the basket that she brought inside the building. It was almost getting boring, except that every time I thought about Ashley and how sweet and precious she was, I got shivery all over.

"Oh, Jana. I'd give anything if something like that would happen to me," said Melanie in a dreamy voice. "It must have been wonderful." Melanie had a look of rapture on her face which isn't unusual. She's a very romantic person.

"But why did Taffy Sinclair, *of all people*, have to be the one with you?" Christie said. "Couldn't you have just died when *she* got some of the credit for finding Ashley?"

"If I had been you, I would have grabbed Ashley away from Taffy and run somewhere where she couldn't find me," said Beth. "She always thinks she's so smart! That would have shown her a thing or two."

I shrugged, but I didn't say anything. My friends were right in a way. Taffy Sinclair and I have been enemies forever. Terrible enemies. But it had been different when Taffy and I were all alone in the hallway with Ashley. It was almost as if we weren't enemies anymore because we were sharing something special. Something wonderful. Still, I didn't really understand it myself, so how could I ever explain it to my friends?

"Well, anyway we're going to have our picture in the *Bridgeport Post* tonight," I said proudly. "And you'll get to see Ashley. Taffy and I held her between us while the photographer took the picture. She's the most beautiful baby in the world."

"I wonder how anyone could just abandon her like that," Melanie said. "She must have a terrible mother."

"Maybe she is sick or on drugs or something and can't take care of her," Katie offered.

"Then why didn't she give Ashley to somebody instead of leaving her out in the cold weather in a basket?" Beth demanded. "She could have frozen to death."

Fortunately, just then the bell rang, ending recess. I didn't want to talk about Ashley's mother and why she had left her baby in a basket on the front steps of the school. I had been trying to keep those thoughts from creeping into my mind ever since Taffy and I found Ashley this morning. They made me uncomfortable and more scared than ever about what was going to happen to her.

At lunchtime, Taffy and I were the stars of the cafeteria. Even though we didn't sit at the same table, I could see that she was getting the same kind of attention I was. Even little first-graders were coming up to me and asking things like, "Did you have to change the baby's diaper?" or "Did she cry until you picked her up the way my baby brother does?" A few kids looked at me sort of funny. I didn't understand why until one of them asked, "Did the baby pull out a handful of your hair?" I thought I'd die, and from then on I tried to lean on my left elbow and casually cover the hole in my hair with my hand.

A couple of times when I looked at Taffy, she was looking back, and we smiled at each other. It felt a little weird to be smiling at Taffy Sinclair, but when I looked at her I couldn't help thinking about the two of us holding baby Ashley, and I had to smile at her. Fortunately the rest of The Fabulous Five didn't notice. They would have had a fit.

It was fun being a celebrity, and the rest of the day went by pretty fast. I hated for it to end, so I wasn't in any rush to get home and sort of poked along. The minute I opened our apartment door the telephone started ringing. Maybe it was Herb Little from the *Bridgeport Post* and he wanted to interview me some more, I thought as I pitched my books on the sofa and dove for the phone.

It wasn't. It was Mom.

"I'm so glad you're home. I just saw your picture in this evening's edition. Everyone here at the paper is talking about what you girls did. Honey, I'm so proud of you!"

Mom is classified ad manager at the *Bridgeport Post*, so naturally she and the other people who work there see the paper before it's delivered to anyone else. I could tell by the sound of her voice that she really meant it when she said she was proud of me, and I had to clear the lump out of my throat before I could answer her.

"Gosh, Mom. You should have seen Ashley. She's the most beautiful baby in the world. And she really loves Taffy and me. She smiled at us all the time, and she tried to put my finger into her mouth until I gave her a bottle."

"She looks beautiful in the picture," Mom assured me. "And there's an article about how you girls found her on the front steps. I'm going to bring home some extra copies so that we can send one to Grandma and to Aunt Carolyn in Ohio, and you can even send one to your father if you want to."

My parents have been divorced since I was three, and my father lives in Poughkeepsie, New York. The mention of him made my heart skip a beat, and I was so busy thinking about how proud he would feel when he read the article and saw my picture that I wasn't prepared for what Mom said next.

"That reminds me, Pink is coming over for dinner tonight to celebrate our decision to get married. Isn't it wonderful, sweetheart? Now we have two things to celebrate."

5 ✻

After we hung up I sat down on the sofa and stared at the phone. How could Mom do this to me? Finding Ashley had made this the most wonderful day of my life, and now she was spoiling it. I didn't want to celebrate Mom and Pink's getting married. It isn't that I don't like Pink. I like him a lot. He's a printer at the newspaper where Mom works, and they've been dating for ages. But why couldn't things just stay the way they are? Pink is an absolute bowling nut, and he has tons of trophies. He could still take Mom bowling every Saturday night, the way he does now, and bring me a deep-dish pepperoni, green pepper, and mushroom pizza before they went out. That would be fine. But even though I had told Mom that I thought it would be great for her and Pink to get married *someday*, I hadn't meant right now!

I was also thinking about my father. I could hardly wait for him to see my picture in the paper. I knew that he would be superproud of me. He would probably call me long-distance to congratulate me or even come to see me. The idea excited me so much that I got an envelope out of the drawer where Mom keeps stationery, pencils, rubber bands, and stuff, and addressed it to him. I would mail it on my way to school in the morning. Just then Mom got home. She came into the apartment, waving the newspaper and grinning like crazy.

"Look, honey. Here's your picture. On the front page!"

She was right. We were on the front page. Taffy Sinclair, baby Ashley, and me. I looked closely at myself first. I looked okay. At least the hole in my hair didn't show. Then I looked at Ashley. She was smiling and waving a little hand in the air. She looked almost as beautiful in the picture as she did in real life. Finally I glanced at Taffy Sinclair. At first I thought that she looked perfect—as usual—but then I noticed that she was smiling so big that you could see her one crooked bicuspid.

Mom was reading the headline out loud. *"TWO SIXTH-GRADERS FIND BABY GIRL ABANDONED ON SCHOOL STEPS."*

I zeroed in on it and followed along as Mom continued to read, *"Authorities are searching for the parents of a five-month-old baby girl found abandoned on the front steps of Mark Twain Elementary School this morning. A handwritten note pinned to her blanket identified her only as Ashley.*

"Sixth-grade students Taffy Sinclair and Jana Morgan were walking in the hallway past the front door of the school when Miss Sinclair spotted the basket containing the baby outside the glass doors and brought the child inside, where she was taken into the principal's office and the police notified.

"Authorities ask that anyone with information as to the identity of the child or the whereabouts of her parents contact police headquarters immediately."

"MISS SINCLAIR!" I shrieked. "What about me? I'm the one who heard her crying! I'm just as important as Taffy! She wouldn't have even looked out the front doors if I hadn't made her stop and listen." I couldn't believe it. Taffy must have said something to Herb Little to make him think that she found Ashley practically single-handedly. I had been stupid to think anything was different between us. She hadn't changed. She was still just as much my enemy as ever.

Mom gave me a reassuring smile. "I'm sure anyone reading the article will understand that you had just as much to do with finding Ashley as Taffy did." She was trying to make me feel better, but it wasn't working.

It was true that Taffy Sinclair and I had been enemies and in competition for things as long as I could remember, but I couldn't help thinking about how we had stopped being enemies the instant we found Ashley.

The whole time we were in the hall with her, it was almost as if we were friends. So why was she always taking the credit for herself? And why had she done it where everyone in the whole wide world would see it— on the front page of the *Bridgeport Post*!

Mom started to head for the kitchen when she stopped and turned back to me again. She had a puzzled look on her face.

"Honey." She paused as if she were searching for the right words. "I see you've changed your hair. Is it something I should know about? You know, a club initiation or something like that?"

I couldn't help but laugh out loud. She was trying her best not to tell me how awful it looked. I shook my head. "I forgot to spit out my gum before I went to bed last night. That's all."

Her look turned sympathetic, and suddenly I felt miserable again. "What am I going to do? Everyone is looking at me. I feel like a jerk!"

"Come on. Let's see what we can do." She led me into the bathroom and began brushing the right side of my hair like crazy. "I wish I could make an appointment for you with Nan, but the truth is, we're almost out of cash. I had to pay the rent on Monday."

I sighed. Nan could fix my hair if anybody could. She's our beautician and she's really super. Then I looked into the mirror at what Mom was doing and felt instantly better. She had brushed the right side behind that ear and was fastening it back with a silver barrette.

"Wow!" I said. "That looks great." Both sides looked practically the same. Anyone would have to really look hard to see that one side was cut off and the other pulled back. "Thanks a million," I said, giving her a big squeeze.

When Pink arrived a little while later, he didn't even notice that my hair was different. He was all smiles, as usual. He is tall and thin with blond hair, and he is always smiling. "I think it's wonderful that you and your friend rescued that poor little baby this morning," he said. "I want to hear all about it."

I forgot about my anger at Taffy Sinclair when he said that, and we sat down in the living room and I told him the whole story. I made sure he understood how it really happened, not the way Taffy was telling it.

Over dinner we talked about Ashley some more. I finally brought up the subject that had been bothering me all day. "Her mother must be a pretty terrible person to leave her out in the cold just in a basket like that."

"Maybe her mother had some kind of problem and couldn't take care of her," Pink said gently.

I didn't say anything for a minute. Why was everybody making excuses for her, I wondered. It didn't make sense.

"You would never have abandoned me when I was a baby, would you, Mom? No matter how many problems you had?"

Mom looked at me and I saw tears flash in her eyes. Then she reached out and put her hand over mine. "No, sweetheart. Of course not. Nothing could ever have made me abandon you."

We were pretty quiet for the rest of the meal. I guess Mom and Pink were thinking about Ashley, but I was thinking about someone else—my father. In a way, I'd have to say that he abandoned me too. I thought about all the times I had wondered why he never came to see me since they were divorced. He almost never wrote me letters, either. I also thought about how often I had wished that he and my mom were still together. Poor Ashley, I thought. I knew how she would feel when she got old enough to understand what had happened.

When we finished eating Mom excused me to do my homework. It wasn't until I was in my room that I realized we hadn't talked about their getting married. I suppose Ashley had taken their minds off that subject.

I went to bed after I finished my homework. Pink was still there. I could hear soft voices coming from the living room. I was too sleepy to care that they were probably talking about their wedding. It had been an exciting day, and I was exhausted.

I awoke with a start sometime later. Mom was touching my shoulder and whispering my name. "Hmmm?" I murmured as I tried to open my eyes.

"I'm sorry to wake you, honey, but the eleven o'clock news is coming on. They said they're going to have a story about you and Taffy and Ashley."

The instant she said that I was wide-awake, and I sprang out of bed and raced to the living room just as the last commercial was over. The next shot was of the news desk and the anchorwoman, who was reporting the day's events.

She looked straight into the camera and said, "Our top story tonight concerns a five-month-old baby girl abandoned on the front steps of Mark Twain Elementary School this morning and found by two sixth-graders passing by the door."

I held my breath as she told the whole story. Mom and I grinned at each other when she said my name, but then we got serious again when she started talking about Ashley.

"Police have turned up no clues to the identity of the baby. A note pinned to her blanket identified her only as Ashley. A check of local hospitals failed to find any record of a baby girl named Ashley born around that time. Doctors examining the baby today discovered a small bruise on her stomach, leading to speculation that she may have been abused before she was abandoned, and authorities are making an urgent appeal for any information on the baby or her parents."

"Abused!" I cried. "Mom! She said Ashley was abused."

"She said *maybe*," Mom said firmly. "They don't know for sure. They just found a bruise, and they have to assume the worst for her own protection."

I thought about that for a moment. Mom was right. They were only taking care of her. Still, the idea of

Ashley's being abused made me feel terrible. Suddenly I got this great idea and my spirits soared again.

"Mom! The police officers who came to the school to get Ashley said that Taffy and I could visit her in her foster home. Tomorrow would you call Officer Martin and find out where the foster home is and get permission for me to visit? Oh, please, Mom. Will you do it?"

Mom smiled softly. "Of course I will."

I had a hard time going back to sleep. I lay there for a long time thinking about how much Ashley and I had in common and what it was going to be like to see her again. Then I made a solemn promise. Nobody would ever abuse her again. I would see to that . . . somehow.

6

I had barely gotten onto the school ground the next morning when kids started running up and telling me they had seen my picture in the paper or their parents had heard about Taffy and me on TV. A couple said they had actually stayed up and watched the late news. I was flabbergasted. I felt like a rock star.

A lot of the little kids from the lower grades just stared at me with their mouths open as I walked by, although I heard a few of them say things like "There she is!" or "There's one of the girls who found the baby!" It felt good to be looked up to.

I headed for the spot where most of the sixth-graders congregate to wait for the bell. Taffy Sinclair was talking to Lisa Snow and Sara Sawyer, and Randy was hanging around with Scott Daly and Mark Peters. Randy saw me coming and gave me his 1,000-watt smile. My four best friends were already there also, and they started giggling when they saw Randy smile at me. Just as I got near them, someone came up behind me and tapped me on the shoulder.

"Jana. Can I talk to you a minute?"

I gritted my teeth and turned around to face Curtis Trowbridge. Leave it to Curtis to follow me around like a lost puppy, I thought. Curtis is a nice person, but unfortunately he is the nerd of the world. He has had a crush on me for ages, which explains why he looks for any excuse to talk to me. This time he was waving the clipping about Taffy and me finding baby Ashley and grinning like crazy.

"Hi, Jana," he said. "I saved your picture out of the paper, and I was wondering if I could have your autograph."

"My autograph?" I repeated in absolute disbelief. I knew that my mouth was hanging open, but I couldn't help it. Only a nerd like Curtis would ask somebody in his own class for an autograph. The other sixth-graders standing nearby were watching and some were even snickering. I was so embarrassed I thought I'd die.

"Sure, Curtis," I mumbled. "I'll do it later, though. I don't have a pencil with me right now."

I started to walk away, but I should have known that Curtis wouldn't give up that easily. He's the original Boy Scout. Always prepared.

"I brought a ballpoint pen," he shouted gleefully. He handed me the pen and then whirled around, slapping the clipping onto his shoulder. "And you can write on my back!"

I think I must have groaned out loud when he did that. The situation was just too gross for words. I took the pen, stepped forward, and scribbled "Your friend, Jana Morgan" as quickly as I could and handed the pen and the clipping back over his shoulder to him. "Here you go, Curtis. I'll see you later. I have to talk to my friends now."

Christie, Beth, Melanie, and Katie were waiting for me by the front door. They were all trying hard not to laugh.

"Come on, guys," I said. "Give me a break. What was I supposed to do? Curtis Trowbridge is the most UNCOOL person in the world. Besides, how many times has any of you been asked for your autograph?" That sent them into hysterical laughter. Changing the subject, I said, "It's time for the bell. We'd better go."

The first thing that I noticed when we got to the classroom was that Wiggins had thumbtacked the article with the picture of Taffy and Ashley and me up on the bulletin board by the front door.

"Hey, Morgan. Way to go," shouted Clarence Marshall as I made my way to my seat. I waved at him and gave him a big smile. Out of the corner of my eye I could see that Randy was looking at me, too. My heart was turning flip-flops, but I managed to flash him a big smile.

Wiggins took roll, but then instead of telling us to get out our math books, she got a serious look on her face and said, "This morning we have a little extra business to conduct. As you know, we have two people in our room who did something very special yesterday. Jana Morgan and Taffy Sinclair, who rescued baby Ashley."

My eyes shot open wide, and I glanced nervously at Taffy. She was looking at me, too, but this time we didn't exchange smiles. Everyone else in the room was nodding and saying yes and pretending to applaud so much that Wiggins finally held up her hand for order.

"The police are looking for clues to the identity of baby Ashley's parents, and they have requested that the teachers ask their classes if anyone saw any person loitering near the school ground yesterday morning before the bell. It is very important that they locate the person who left the baby on the steps. Think hard, now. If any of you saw anyone sitting in a car or walking near the school or doing anything unusual, please raise your hand."

Nobody could remember seeing anyone suspicious, and after a while Wiggins said that if anyone thought of anything later, he or she should come up to her desk and tell her. Then we started our math lesson.

In the cafeteria at noon I nibbled on my cream cheese and jelly sandwich and thought about Ashley. I wondered how she was today, and I wished more than anything that I would get to see her soon. I also thought about the bruise that the doctors had found on her stomach, and all of a sudden I had a hard time swallowing the bite of sandwich in my mouth.

"Did you know that they think Ashley may have been abused?" I asked.

"You're kidding," said Christie. "How do you know?"

"It was on the eleven o'clock news last night," I said. "The doctors who examined her found a small bruise on her stomach." Then in a softer voice I added, "They think her mother may have done it before she abandoned her."

Beth looked disgusted. "Some mother!"

"They don't know for sure that's how the bruise got there," I said. "But they really want to talk to Ashley's mother badly or to anyone else who might know anything."

"I'll bet she's a druggie," said Katie. "They do crazy things when they're high."

We all nodded solemnly, and then Melanie said, "Will they give her back to her mother when they find her?"

The question startled me. "I don't know," I confessed. "I never thought about that."

"I bet they won't," said Melanie. "Not if she abused Ashley."

I wanted to agree with Melanie, but I wasn't sure. Things were getting awfully complicated. Now it was more important than ever to get to see Ashley. I wondered if Mom had called the police department yet. What if they changed their minds and wouldn't let me see her? Mom wouldn't let them do that. She understood how important Ashley was to me. But what if she couldn't do anything about it? I still had the whole afternoon to go before Mom and I both got home and I could find out what the police said. How would I stand it until then?

7 ✳

The first thing I noticed when I left the cafeteria with my friends was that Taffy Sinclair had cornered Curtis Trowbridge in the hall and was talking his ear off. Aside from being the nerd of the world, he is also sixth-grade editor of our school newspaper, the *Mark Twain Sentinel*, and I knew that was why Taffy was talking to him. She wanted all the publicity she could get.

"Just look at that," Beth snapped. "I'll bet she's telling him that *she* was the one who found Ashley, and that she did it all by herself. Otherwise she wouldn't be caught dead talking to a nerd like Curtis. What are you going to do, Jana?"

"I don't know." I was fuming, but I would rather have died than let Taffy Sinclair know it. "Keep on walking as if you don't even see them," I instructed.

All five of us raised our noses into the air and strolled past as if we couldn't be bothered to look at Taffy. A moment later I heard someone clattering up the hallway behind us.

"Wait up, Jana. I need to talk to you again." It was Curtis.

"Oh, hi, Curtis," I said, pretending to be really surprised to see him.

"I have decided to do a story on you and Taffy finding the abandoned baby for this Friday's *Sentinel*. I just talked to Taffy about how she found the baby, and I was wondering if I could interview you and get your part of the story."

I considered the situation for a moment. He had just talked to Taffy about how *she* found the baby, huh? Big deal. And now he wanted to hear my *part* of the story, as if I had hardly anything to do with finding Ashley. On the other hand, it was me that Curtis had a crush on, and he was gazing at me with such a lovesick expression that you would have thought he had just proposed. I knew that if I wanted to, I could really get even with Taffy Sinclair. A sly smile drifted across my face. I wanted to.

"Sure, Curtis," I purred. "Let's go somewhere private where we can talk."

❀ ❀ ❀

I had been right about the afternoon lasting forever. Then once I got home from school, I had another hour to wait for Mom to get off work. I couldn't sit still. I had to know about Ashley. I was pacing the floor when I heard Mom's key turn in the lock.

"Hi, sweetheart," she said as I raced to meet her.

"What did they say? The police, I mean. Did you ask them about my visiting Ashley?"

"Whoa!" Mom said good-naturedly. "Give me a chance to catch my breath and hang up my coat."

It seemed to take forever for Mom to hang up her coat. I trailed her like an anxious puppy, only I wanted to be answered instead of scratched behind the ears. Mom finally turned to look at me. Then she sighed. Uh-oh, I thought. Trouble.

"I called the police station this morning," she began "and I talked to Officer Martin. At first she said she was sorry, but that you wouldn't be able to see Ashley at all."

"But, Mom!" I protested. I knew I was interrupting, but this was critical. "Officer Martin said I could. She promised!"

"Let me finish," Mom said sternly. "She said because Ashley may have been abused, they have to keep her whereabouts a secret. They can't take a chance on that person finding her and hurting her again. They know that you would never hurt her or tell anyone where she is, but they can't make any exceptions. You understand that, don't you, Jana?"

Of course I understood a thing like that. I nodded, but I couldn't speak around the lump in my throat.

"Then Officer Martin talked to someone in the department who is handling Ashley's case and called me back. She said that they understand how special Ashley is to you, and they have agreed that you can come to the police station Saturday afternoon at two o'clock. They'll bring Ashley from her foster home, and you'll be able to see her then."

"Whoopee!" I shrieked, zooming into Mom's open arms and hugging her tightly. "Oh, Mom. You've got to come with me. You've got to see Ashley. She's the most beautiful baby in the world."

"I think we can arrange that." Mom was pretending to be serious, but her eyes were shining as she looked down at me.

Then it was my turn to be serious. "What if they find Ashley's mother and she *was* the one who abused her? Will they give Ashley back to her?" I pulled out of Mom's arms and looked pleadingly at her. "They wouldn't, would they?"

Mom thought for a moment. "I'm sure they wouldn't. Not if they could prove she was the one who abused Ashley, but that might be hard to do. I suppose the court would have to decide. But let's not worry about that now," she said, brightening. "They haven't found her mother yet, and we are going to get to see her on Saturday."

"Okay," I promised. Then my spirits sagged again. "But this is only Wednesday. Anything could happen by then."

Something did happen later that evening, but it wasn't what I had expected. The phone rang about seven o'clock. I was doing my homework in my room, but Mom was watching TV on the sofa next to the phone, so she answered it. I thought it must have been for her since she didn't call me. I went on reading my social studies chapter and didn't pay much attention to what she was saying. A couple of minutes later she came tearing into my room.

"Jana! You'll never guess who was just on the phone."

I looked at her blankly and shook my head.

"It was Marge Whitworth from the television station. She's the one who reported the story about you and Taffy on last night's news. She wants to interview both of you for TV!"

"Oh, my gosh! I don't believe it." By now I was standing up, dancing around my desk. "What did she say? Didn't she want to talk to me?"

"She will later, sweetheart. First she wanted to get my permission for you to be interviewed. Of course I said yes. I knew you'd love to do it. Then she said she'd check her schedule and get back to us to set up a time to tape the interview. It won't be part of the regular newscast. This will be a special feature story about you and Taffy as individuals. She'll talk to each of you about what you are like. How it felt to find an abandoned baby. Things like that. She called it the human-interest angle. Isn't this exciting? My little girl is going to be on TV!"

It *was* exciting. I had never dreamed of being on television in my whole life until this moment. Marge Whitworth called back a little later and talked to Mom again. She said that she would like me to be at the television station at four o'clock Saturday afternoon. Mom said we could go straight there from seeing Ashley. Saturday was going to be the most fabulous day of my life. I was not only going to get to see the most wonderful baby in the world again, I was going to be on TV! I was so excited I thought I'd die.

After I called the rest of The Fabulous Five and told them the great news, I spent the rest of the evening trying to imagine me—Jana Morgan—on TV. It was hard. I could get a picture in my mind of the television set and of Marge Whitworth reporting the news. I'd seen that tons of times. But every time I tried to visualize myself on the screen next to Ms. Whitworth, I went blank. I wondered what it would be like. My heart started to pound at the thought of it.

Of course, Taffy Sinclair had already been on television when she had had that teensy little part in the soap opera *Interns and Lovers*. But she didn't get to say anything. Still, I knew she would act like a big authority and try to tell me what to do. Well, I wouldn't let her get away with a thing like that. I would tell her where to get off!

Mom said Marge Whitworth was going to ask us questions about finding Ashley. I was already starting to get nervous. Would I have stage fright? Would I stutter or say the words wrong? And what about my hair? Even though Mom was letting me use her silver barrette, would the hole show anyway?

"*O*h, Jana," squealed Beth, when I got to school the next morning. "I'm so jealous of you that I could just die. I'd give anything to be on TV!"

"Aren't you scared?" asked Melanie. She was the one who looked scared. Her eyes were wide and her mouth was sort of quivery. "When you look into that camera, you'll know that thousands—maybe even millions—of people will be watching."

"Oh brother." Katie moaned. "It's just a local newscast, and she'll probably only be on for a couple of minutes. It isn't as if she were going to be a star or anything."

"Well, I'd STILL be scared!" huffed Melanie.

"I am a little nervous," I confessed as we started walking toward the building. "I mean, it is my first time on television . . . not like SOME people we know."

Just as my friends and I were exchanging knowing glances, Taffy Sinclair's icky sweet voice rang out from the crowd of sixth-graders just in front of us.

". . . and Marge Whitworth is going to interview ME on television and ask me all sorts of questions about finding baby Ashley. She's going to interview Jana, too, of course, about thinking she heard a kitten crying when it was really a baby." Taffy laughed as if she had just made the biggest joke in the world, and giggles swept through the crowd of kids.

Nobody had seen us walk up. We stopped when we heard Taffy's voice, and I just stood there for a moment feeling angry. How could she do this to me after what we had been through together? She was making me look like the world's biggest idiot in front of my class.

Just then I heard another voice. "Hey, Jana. Is it true that you're going to be on TV?" It was Randy Kirwan, walking by with his best friends, Scott Daly and Mark Peters. My hand flew up to my left ear, hiding the hole in my hair. Then I looked at him, and he was giving me his 1,000-watt smile.

"That's right," I said proudly. "We're going to tape the interview on Saturday afternoon, and it will be on television that night."

"Wow!" He had turned around and was walking backwards so that he could still look at me as he went past. "You're going to be famous!"

I wanted to say something cool, like, "Oh, it's nothing. Just a little television interview," but when I rehearsed it in my mind it sounded awfully phony so I just smiled back at him and sort of shrugged.

But Taffy Sinclair wasn't finished with me yet. She and Mona Vaughn were standing just outside the cafeteria door at noon. My friends had already gone in, but I had stopped by the drinking fountain and was hurrying to catch up. I could tell that Taffy and Mona were waiting for someone, but I didn't know at first that it was me. Just as I reached out to open the cafeteria door, Taffy stepped up.

"You aren't really going to appear on television with your hair like that, are you?" she asked smugly.

My hand shot up to cover my left ear. I was wearing Mom's barrette, and I had been confident that no one would notice the hole. "What do you mean 'like that'?" I demanded.

Her eyes narrowed. "You know exactly what I mean. You may not care what you look like, but I'll be mortified if you show up on the same program I'm on with hair over one ear and a hole over the other. You may think you can hide it by wearing that barrette, but you can't. It looks awful!"

"I thought I explained to you that this is the latest style! But I guess you just don't keep up with fashion." Then I stuck my nose into the air and marched into the cafeteria.

When I told my friends what Taffy had said, they got mad, too.

"The nerve of that Taffy Sinclair," Katie said between clenched teeth. "Who does she think she is, anyway?"

"You can't let her get away with a thing like that," said Christie.

"Yeah," said Beth. "What are you going to do?"

I looked blankly at Beth. "What am I going to do?" I echoed. "What CAN I do? I can't grow hair over my left ear by the day after tomorrow."

"No . . ." said Melanie slowly. "But there is something you could do. In fact, I'd be willing to help you."

"What's that?" I asked eagerly.

"Well," she said, studying me for a moment, "I think just a little trimming could even up the sides of your hair so that nobody would even notice the hole."

"Hey. She's right," said Beth. "I'll help."

"Me, too," offered Christie. "My aunt Helen is a beautician and fixing hair runs in our family."

"Great!" I said. "Can you guys come home with me after school? I can't wait to get this mess straightened out."

When we got to my apartment, my friends were all excited about trimming my hair. "Get the scissors and a towel and sit at the kitchen table," instructed Christie.

"I think we'd better spread some newspaper around the floor to catch the hair," said Katie.

"Hey, wait a minute," I said with a laugh. "You're just going to even up my hair. You're not going to shave my head." My friends all laughed too.

I got some newspapers, anyway, deciding it would be easier to catch bits of hair now than run the vacuum cleaner later. Then I got out the scissors, wrapped a pink bath towel around my shoulders, and sat down at the kitchen table.

"It was my idea so I get to go first," shouted Melanie.

"No fair," said Christie. "I'm the one with the natural talent. Remember? My aunt is a beautician."

I was starting to get nervous. "Come on. Somebody do something. Let's get this over with."

Melanie swooped forward and grabbed the scissors off the table before anyone else could get them. Then she pushed the right side of my face a little bit, tilting my head. "There," she said. "Hold that position."

"That's crooked," protested Beth. "One side will be longer than the other."

"No, it won't," insisted Melanie.

"Maybe I should look in a mirror while you do this," I offered. I was beginning to wonder if this had been such a super idea after all.

Melanie got a grief-stricken look on her face. "Don't you trust me?" she whispered.

I felt like a villain. I didn't want to hurt her feelings so I just shrugged and said, "Sure."

I didn't have to wait long. There was this incredibly loud WHACK! just beside my right ear.

"That's too short!" shrieked Beth even before a big glob of hair fell onto my shoulder. "You've cut it wrong. Here. Give me those scissors."

Grabbing the scissors away from Melanie and tilting my head the other direction, Beth began to cut in tiny snip-snip-snips on the left side.

"Why are you cutting there?" I demanded. "That's where the hole is."

"I told you that Melanie cut it too short," said Beth. "I'm just evening it up."

I was definitely starting to panic. "I think I ought to see it now," I insisted. "Somebody bring me a mirror."

"Take it easy, Jana," said Christie. "It's looking great. There are just a couple of spots that need working on. I know how to do it too. I've watched my aunt Helen cut hair hundreds of time. Give me the scissors now."

Reluctantly Beth handed Christie the scissors. There was another WHACK! and a huge chunk of hair dropped into the right side of my lap. "Whoops!" said Christie.

I thought I'd die. "Why did you say 'Whoops!'?" I cried. "I want to see my hair!" I struggled to get up, but four pairs of hands held me down.

"We aren't through yet," said Katie.

"Please, Jana," begged Melanie. "Don't look yet. Not until we're all finished. You'll like it. I promise."

My heart was pounding in an irregular beat, keeping time with the snip of the scissors. What were they doing to me? And why had I let them? I was dying to look at myself, but I was also afraid to. They had gotten awfully quiet as they passed the scissors back and forth, first one and then another cutting off a piece of my hair.

Every so often they would stop, stand back, and look at me as if I were a bug under a microscope. Then they would start cutting again.

Finally they stopped and got into a sort of huddle like football players deciding which play to run next. Little tingles of fear raced up my spine. I wanted to ask them what they were talking about, but I couldn't. After a minute, they turned toward me. Not one of them was smiling.

"Uh . . ." Melanie began. "It really doesn't look TOO terrible."

"We did the best we could," added Beth.

I stood up. I let the towel fall from my shoulders without even thinking about all the hair dropping onto the floor. Then I raced into the bathroom and stared into the mirror. "My hair!" I shrieked. "You cut off all my hair!"

I didn't recognize the person staring back at me. Surely it wasn't me, the girl with dark brown hair to her shoulders. It wasn't even the girl with the hole in her hair. There was only a little stubble over each ear. The back was shorter too, chopped off in layers like upside-down stairsteps. It was the worst-looking haircut I had ever seen.

My friends were lined up behind me looking miserable.

"We're sorry," mumbled Katie. "We were only trying to help."

"I guess I didn't learn as much from watching my aunt Helen as I thought," Christie said.

"What are you going to do now?" asked Beth.

I leaned my forehead against the mirror and closed my eyes. "Chicken out," I whispered. "Taffy Sinclair can do the interview by herself. I'd absolutely die before I'd be seen on TV like this."

9 ❀

*T*he first thing I did after my friends left was get a brown paper grocery bag from under the kitchen sink. Halfway up one side I cut eyeholes and slipped the bag over my head. Then I made a solemn promise to wear that bag for the rest of my life.

As Katie had said, my friends were only trying to help. But the truth of the matter was, they had ruined me. Destroyed my hair. Turned me into a freak. I could never show my face—or my hair—in public again.

Then I sat down at the kitchen table and stared into space, thinking about Taffy Sinclair. My friends couldn't have done anything to make her happier. Now she could go on television and say anything she wanted to about baby Ashley. She could tell the whole world that I was too stupid to know the difference between a kitten crying and a baby, and I wouldn't be there to set the story straight. Everyone would think I was a jerk.

Suddenly I heard Mom's key turn in the lock. I didn't know how I was going to tell her that I wasn't going to be on television. She had been so proud of me when Marge Whitworth called. I could only hope that she would understand.

"Hi, Jana," she said in her usual cheerful voice. "How was your . . ." Mom stopped in mid-sentence. I could see the instant surprise in her eyes when she saw me with the brown paper bag over my head. ". . . day?" she finished softly.

"Rotten," I grumbled. My voice echoed inside the bag.

Mom didn't say anything while she hung up her coat. I knew she was trying to figure out what to do next.

"Would you like to talk about it?" she asked.

"No." That wasn't really the truth, but I still didn't know what to say.

Mom nodded as if to say that she understood and came into the kitchen. She got out two tall glasses, filled them with instant tea, water, and ice cubes. "Care to join me?" she asked casually as she sat down across from me and held a glass out toward me.

It was getting awfully stuffy inside that paper bag, and I hadn't taken time for a snack or a drink when I had gotten home. I mumbled thank-you and took the iced tea from her. Suddenly the hand holding the glass stopped in midair. I had cut eye holes but no mouth hole. How was I going to drink my iced tea? Or eat my dinner? I thought about pushing the glass up inside the bag, but that wouldn't work. Even if I got it up to my mouth, how would I tip it far enough to take a drink without punching a hole in the bag?

Sighing, I set the glass back down on the table. "I have a problem. And I've made up my mind, so don't try to talk me out of it. I'm not going to be on TV."

Mom dumped a packet of artificial sweetener into her tea and stirred it before she said anything. "And does this problem have anything to do with the hole in your hair?"

"It's worse than that!" The tears that had been threatening to flood my eyes ever since my friends left came bursting through as if a dam had broken. "Just LOOK!" I sobbed as I tore the paper bag off my head.

Mom can usually fake it and remain cool through any situation, but this time her mouth dropped open, and she made a gasping sound. "Oh, no," she cried. "Oh, Jana. What happened?"

I swiped away the tears with the back of my hand and cleared my throat. Then I told her the whole story, beginning with Taffy's saying that she would be embarrassed to be on the same TV program with me if I had a hole in my hair and ending with my friends trying to help by giving me a haircut.

"It was free," I added, trying to end on a hopeful note.

"Oh, sweetheart." Mom opened her arms wide and I hurried to her to get a hug. "It's going to be okay. I promise. Now let me make a phone call."

Mom dialed the phone, and when someone answered on the other end she asked for Nan.

"Hi, Nan," she said a few seconds later. "This is Pat Morgan. Could you possibly change my daughter's haircut appointment for tomorrow after school to today? This is a real emergency."

I sucked in my breath. I couldn't believe it. She had said we couldn't afford to have my hair cut, and now she was changing an appointment for tomorrow to today.

"Uh-hm," Mom said, nodding and grinning at me while she talked. "Wonderful. We'll be right there. And, Nan. Thanks a million."

On the way Mom explained that she had decided that I really did need to have the hole in my hair fixed. She had made the appointment for Friday after school because Friday was payday, and she had planned to surprise me.

"Don't worry," she said when she saw the concern on my face. "I'm sure Nan will let me pay her tomorrow."

Nan did a super job on my hair. She layered the back so that the upside-down stairsteps didn't show, trimmed it all over to even it up, and then showed me how to style it by feathering it back away from my face. I had seen this style in teen magazines dozens of times. It was fantastic. In fact, I looked better than I had ever looked before. Taffy Sinclair, I thought with a grin, would absolutely die if she knew that she was partly responsible for my terrific new look.

When my friends saw me at school the next morning, they nearly fainted with relief.

"Oh, Jana!" Beth said, leaning against a tree as if she couldn't stand up by herself. "It looks great! I've been so worried. I thought you'd never speak to me again."

"Me, too," said Melanie. "I cried all night just thinking about what we did to your hair."

"It's okay," I said. "In fact, I like it better this way."

I got admiring glances from everybody, including Randy Kirwan. Only Taffy Sinclair was upset. She took one look at me when I passed her on the school ground and stormed off toward the door.

I had almost forgotten about my interview with Curtis Trowbridge for the *Mark Twain Sentinel* until Wiggins handed out the paper right after she took roll and made the morning announcements. The headline was nothing special:

SIXTH-GRADERS FIND BABY

But the article was so great that it made me want to break-dance on the top of my desk. Today was definitely my day. It began: *"Thanks to the keen ears of Jana Morgan, a tiny baby known only as Ashley was saved from freezing to death on the front steps of Mark Twain Elementary on Tuesday morning."*

It went on to say that Taffy and I were walking down the hall when I heard a sound and insisted that we both look around. It did say that Taffy brought Ashley inside the building, of course, but *then* it said the best part of all. Good old Curtis Trowbridge. He wrote it just the way I told him: "*When Ashley grabbed Jana's finger and started pulling it toward her mouth, Jana alertly realized that the baby was hungry. She dug around in the basket and found a bottle of milk. Then she cuddled Ashley in her arms and fed her until she was full and a smiling, happy baby again.*"

It's about time somebody got the story straight, I thought smugly. Curtis is certainly a better reporter than that Herb Little from the *Bridgeport Post*! Then I looked at Taffy Sinclair. Luckily, she sits four seats in front of me, up near Wiggins's desk, so I can keep an eye on her without having to turn around. Taffy was twirling a strand of her hair around her finger so furiously while she read the paper that I could almost swear I saw smoke coming out of her ears. For an instant I felt a little guilty. I remembered how special it had been when Taffy and I found Ashley, almost as if we were friends. But she had been going around trying to convince people that she was more important to Ashley than I was. That wasn't true! I was just as important as she was. Now maybe everyone would understand.

10 ✳

The next afternoon Pink picked up Mom and me in his blue Camaro at one-thirty and drove us across town to the police station. It was going to be a super afternoon, and I couldn't decide if I was more excited about seeing Ashley again or being interviewed for television.

"Wow! You look gorgeous," Pink said as I squeezed into the backseat. "And I really like your hair."

"Thanks." I didn't admit it to Pink, but I felt gorgeous. I had picked out my pale blue sweater with the lace collar, which is my favorite and definitely makes me look older. Besides that, Mom had assured me that it would look great on TV. I was also wearing my navy and beige pleated skirt and my new flats with lacy beige anklets.

65

We had scarcely pulled away from the curb when I leaned forward and asked, "Do you think Ashley will remember me?"

Mom smiled at me over the top of her bucket seat. "I'll bet she will," she said happily. "You're a very important person in her life."

I sank back, feeling glad. Then another thought occurred to me. "If she remembers me," I said slowly, "then she'll probably remember her mother . . . and being abused."

Mom's expression clouded. "Oh, dear. I didn't mean that she would REALLY remember you," she said apologetically. "She's too young for that. I just meant that you were able to make her so happy when you found her that I'm sure she'll be happy when she's with you again."

"Then she would NOT be happy with her mother," I persisted. "Right?"

"We don't know that, Jana," said Pink. "Nobody knows if Ashley actually was abused or if that bruise was from an accident."

"Think of all the times you've gotten bruised," Mom interjected. "They were accidents, weren't they?"

"But you didn't abandon me!" I challenged. "Like Beth said, Ashley's mother beat up her baby and then dumped her."

Mom let out an exasperated sigh and looked away from me the way she always does when she decides that she can't reason with me anymore. I knew that I was being unreasonable. I also knew that I should be happy that I was on my way to see Ashley again and to be on television and that my hair looked great. I was happy, but I couldn't help all the other feelings I was having at the same time. I just loved Ashley so much, and I couldn't stand to think of her being hurt again.

Pink pulled the car into the parking lot beside the police station. I wondered if Ashley was already inside. I looked at the big brick building and shuddered. It looked like a prison, not like the sort of place where you would go to visit a baby.

When we got inside, Mom smiled and nudged me toward the main desk. "Go ahead," she said gently. "Tell them who you are. I'm sure they're expecting you."

I looked at Pink. He nodded, and then he gave me a wink and a big smile.

I took a deep breath and approached the front desk. The policeman who looked up from his paperwork smiled at me, and I wondered if he already knew who I was. "My name is Jana Morgan," I said importantly. "I'm here to see Officer Martin and baby Ashley."

"Yes, of course," he said kindly. "Officer Martin is expecting you. If you and your parents would like to follow me, she's in one of the conference rooms."

I blushed when he said "parents" and glanced at Pink, who winked at me again. Of course the policeman had no way of knowing that Pink was Mom's boyfriend and not my father.

Officer Martin opened the conference room door as soon as we knocked. She had a big smile on her face, and I could tell instantly that she was genuinely glad to see me. "Come on in," she said. "Ashley will be here in a couple of minutes."

I introduced Officer Martin to Mom and Pink, and while they talked I looked around the room. There was a big conference table in the middle with about a dozen chairs around it. There was a window looking out onto a street, and on the opposite wall was a green chalkboard. That was it. I sighed and started to fidget. Where was Ashley? What was taking so long?

Just then there was another knock at the door. I sucked in my breath and whirled around. The door opened and there she was, wrapped in a bright pink quilt and being carried by a lady in a brown coat. I didn't look at the lady. All I could see was Ashley. Her eyes were closed, and she was snuggled all cozy and warm in the lady's arms. She was so beautiful with her rosy little cheeks and her tiny, button nose that I thought my heart would burst.

The lady carrying Ashley stepped toward me. "Hello, Jana. I'm Mrs. Ellison, Ashley's foster mother. I'm very glad to meet you." Then she bent forward slightly so that I could get a better look at Ashley.

"Hi," I said without taking my eyes off Ashley's face. "I'm glad to meet you, too."

I don't know if it was the sound of my voice that woke Ashley, but at just that moment she opened her eyes and looked straight at me—and then she smiled. Ashley's smile lit up the whole room. It was as if a million Christmas lights had been switched on. I was glowing, too. I knew I had to be, and I couldn't take my eyes off her face or hear what it was that Mom and the others were saying. It didn't matter. Ashley was here. She was okay, and she was smiling at *me*.

"Would you like to hold her?" Mrs. Ellison said.

I nodded, too filled with the joy of seeing Ashley again to answer.

"Just sit down in one of the chairs," she instructed. "Let me know when you're comfortable, and I'll put Ashley in your arms."

I settled in a chair, then nodded at Mrs. Ellison. The room got very quiet as she gently put Ashley into my waiting arms. She smelled clean and sweet and faintly of talcum powder. She was heavier than I remembered, but I held her tightly. "Hi, Ashley," I said in a chirpy voice. "Remember me?"

Ashley smiled again and made a gurgly sound. Then she pushed her little fist out from her blanket and waved it at me as if she were saying hello. She was glad to see me. I knew she was, whether she remembered exactly what happened when we were together before or not. She knew I was her friend and that she could trust me— forever.

Pink knelt down beside me and stroked Ashley's forehead. She turned her beautiful blue eyes on him and gave him one of her fabulous smiles. He looked so proud you would have thought Ashley was his little girl. For an instant I couldn't help thinking that maybe he would make a pretty good father after all, in spite of how I'd felt before.

"You were right, honey," he said. "Ashley is a beautiful baby. I can see why you love her so much and why you have been so worried about her."

"The two of you must be very proud of Jana," said Officer Martin.

Pink and Mom both nodded and looked down at me. Then Mom asked her the question I was dying to ask. "Have you found Ashley's mother yet?"

Officer Martin shook her head. "I'm afraid not. We've had very few clues to follow, and it doesn't look as if Ashley was born anywhere in this area. We've checked all the birth certificates on file with the state of Connecticut and with every hospital, and nobody has a record of a baby girl named Ashley with a birthday around the time we think she was born. We've checked all the footprint records, too, since they're more accurate than names. Sometimes people change babies' names or don't name them until several days after the birth certificate is recorded. We haven't given up the search, though," she said, looking straight at me. "We'll find someone who knows something. You can count on that."

I nodded, and all the mixed-up feelings I had been having came flooding over me again. Part of me wanted Ashley's mother to be found. And punished for hurting

Ashley. Maybe even put in jail. But another part of me wasn't sure. I looked at Ashley's sunny smile. "I love you," I whispered and held out my finger for her to grab hold of.

Just then another knock sounded at the door. Officer Martin excused herself and went to answer it. It's more police officers wanting to get a look at Ashley, I thought. But when the door opened and I looked up, I got the surprise of my life.

There stood Taffy Sinclair, smiling so big that you could see her one crooked bicuspid, and she was carrying a gigantic teddy bear.

11 *

*P*andemonium broke out in the conference room the minute Taffy Sinclair stepped through the door. She swooped down on Ashley and me, practically smothering Ashley with that stupid teddy bear. At the same time Taffy's mother and father trooped in, pushing Mom and Pink aside and marching over to see Ashley for themselves. They were followed by Marge Whitworth and her entire television crew. I couldn't believe what I was seeing.

I cuddled Ashley to protect her from all the people, but it didn't help. She began to cry. Ashley didn't just cry. She started with a little wail, closing her eyes and screwing up her face into a grimace, and ended up screaming. I rocked her a little bit and patted her and tried to coo in her ear as she wailed away, but she was too upset. And so was I. It was all Taffy Sinclair's fault. She had spoiled everything.

Finally, Mrs. Ellison took Ashley out of my arms and carried her over to a corner, where she was able to quiet her down in spite of all the noise and confusion. Mrs. Sinclair, a brassy blonde who looked a lot like Taffy only older, was talking a mile a minute to Marge Whitworth, telling her how Taffy had once had a part on TV. She's probably trying to get Taffy a television show of her own, I thought with disgust. Taffy's father stood quietly to one side. He was a chubby man with a fringe of dark hair that stretched around the back of his head and hooked over each ear, leaving the top bald and shiny like a mirror.

Officer Martin walked over and looked at me sympathetically. "I guess I forgot to tell you that they were coming. Marge Whitworth called this morning to ask if there were any new developments in the search for Ashley's mother, and I just happened to mention that you were coming to see the baby this afternoon. She got excited about the idea of having you and Taffy and the baby all on television together. Then she offered to call Taffy and her parents and set the whole thing up if we would allow her to tape the interview here at the station."

"Oh," I grumbled. I knew that I shouldn't be mad at Officer Martin. She didn't mean to cause any problems, but why did Taffy Sinclair have to be here? Why did she have to come barging in just when Ashley and I were having such a super time? Ashley had been smiling at me. She didn't start crying until Taffy and all the other people got here.

Out of the corner of my eye I saw that Mrs. Ellison was letting Taffy hold Ashley now that she was quiet again. Everyone else was getting quiet again, too, looking at Taffy as if she were an angel sitting on a cloud. I knew that I shouldn't be jealous since she had helped find Ashley, but I couldn't help it. It didn't seem fair. Taffy always got attention, no matter what she was doing.

"Hi, darling little baby Ashley," Taffy said in her icky sweet voice. "Did you see the BIG present I brought you?"

Behind me I heard Marge Whitworth talking to one of her crew. "Wasn't that thoughtful of Taffy Sinclair?" she was saying. "She brought the baby that beautiful bear."

I didn't listen to her crew member's response. I didn't want to hear it. More than anything I wished that I had brought Ashley a great present. Why didn't I think of it? Nobody, not even Taffy, loved Ashley more than I did.

Just then I felt a hand on my shoulder and looked up. Mom was there, and she was smiling. "Miss Whitworth says you should be getting ready for the interview. They're going to be setting up in a minute. She suggested that you put on a little bit of lip gloss and blush so that you won't look pale under all the lights. I brought some with me. Shall we go to the ladies' room and get you all fixed up?"

I was too choked up to say anything so I nodded and followed her out of the room. When we got back Mrs. Ellison was holding Ashley again, and Taffy was by the chalkboard with her parents, primping in a small mirror. The television crew was scampering everywhere. They had set up enormous lights on tripod legs and had trained them on three chairs at one end of the room. Between two of the chairs was a small table and on top of it was a plastic baby carrier. I guessed that was where Ashley would be during the interview. There was also a tiny microphone, the kind you pin to your clothes, lying on each seat, and the wires coming from them were crisscrossing around the floor. A big man with curly red hair was pulling a heavy black camera out of a box marked "Minicam" and balancing it on one shoulder.

"Okay, Miss Whitworth," he called out. "We're ready when you are."

Marge Whitworth took charge of the scene at once. She was a pretty woman with dark hair falling softly to her shoulders. But she spoke sharply and sounded like a general. She reminded me of Wiggins when she gets angry at our class.

"All right, parents. I'd appreciate absolute silence while the interview is going on. Your daughters and I are going to have a good time, so just relax."

I stole a quick glance at Mom and Pink. It had never occurred to me that they might be nervous, but Mom was shifting uncomfortably from one foot to the other, and Pink was biting on one of his fingernails. I had never seen him do that before. It meant that he cared for me more than I had ever realized. I couldn't help but smile.

"Taffy, you sit on the left side of the table, and Jana, you sit on the right. I'll take this chair." As she said that she pulled her chair a little way away from the other two and angled it so that she was turned toward us. Then she sat down and pinned her mike to her blouse. Taffy and I did the same.

"You're probably nervous, but I'm not," Taffy whispered wickedly. "I'VE been on television before."

"I'm not nervous either," I snapped, even though it was a lie.

Then Miss Whitworth explained to us that they were just making a tape right now and that there would be plenty of time to edit out anything that we didn't want to appear on TV. I supposed she meant that if Ashley started screaming again or if we goofed and said something embarrassing, the whole world wouldn't have to hear it. I was relieved by that. Then she signaled Mrs. Ellison, who brought Ashley over and gently laid her in the baby seat. Ashley was beaming, and when she smiled at me I forgot all about being nervous. "Now, girls, smile," Miss Whitworth said, "and we'll roll the tape."

I did, looking straight at the little red light on the camera as Miss Whitworth started speaking. "Ladies and gentlemen, tonight it is my privilege to present two sixth-graders from Mark Twain Elementary School here in Bridgeport and baby Ashley, the little girl they found abandoned on the school steps last Tuesday morning.

"I'm going to begin this interview by introducing each of them to you. Jana, will you tell us your name and a little bit about yourself?"

When she said my name, I jumped as if someone had jabbed me with a pin. I didn't know that I was going to be first.

"My na . . . my name is Jana Morgan," I began in a shaky voice. "I go to school at Mark Twain Elementary and I'm in the sixth grade." I shot Miss Whitworth a quick grin to let her know that that was all I could think of to say.

She got it. "Thank you, Jana. Now, Taffy. May we hear a little bit about you?"

Taffy looked straight into the camera with a big fake smile on her face. "My name is Taffy Sinclair and I live at nine oh oh seven High Ridge Road with my parents, Mr. and Mrs. Walter Sinclair. In addition to school, I enjoy acting and recently had a part in a daytime drama called *Interns and Lovers* on national TV."

I thought I'd die. "Daytime drama" instead of soap opera! What a snobby thing to say. Besides that, Taffy

Sinclair had practically given her whole life history, and all I had said was that I was in sixth grade at Mark Twain Elementary.

Marge Whitworth was talking again. "I think almost everybody has heard about your experience finding Ashley. But I'd like each of you to tell the audience about it in your own words. Taffy, you begin this time. What happened Tuesday morning?"

Taffy flashed another dazzling smile at the camera. "Well, we were walking in the hall toward the office when Jana told me to stop because she heard a KITTEN crying. I stopped and we both looked around. Then I looked out the glass front doors and saw a basket with a baby in it right there on the steps. I ran out and got it and brought it back inside."

I sat there smoldering. I could hardly wait until my turn to tell everybody how it really happened.

"Jana," Miss Whitworth said, "suppose you tell us how it felt when you realized that it was actually a baby that you had found."

I blinked. This was not what I had expected her to ask me. Then I looked down at Ashley. She was waving a little hand toward me. I felt warm all over and forgot about the camera and even about all the people who would watch us on television. I smiled at Ashley and gave her my finger to hold. She squeezed it tightly. Then I turned toward Miss Whitworth and answered.

"It was the most wonderful moment of my life. Ashley is the most beautiful and most precious baby in the world, and anybody who ever saw her would have to love her. And when Taffy and I first found her all tiny and helpless in her basket, and she smiled at us as if . . ." my voice trailed off. Then I looked at Taffy, and her eyes were shining as if she was remembering too, and she was looking at me as if I were her best friend in the world. "Well," I went on, feeling suddenly embarrassed as if I had told a secret to the world, "it's hard to explain. It was just AWFULLY special."

Marge Whitworth didn't ask us any more questions. She just thanked us and asked again for anyone with information about Ashley to get in touch with the police. Then she signed off.

The first thing I saw when the interview was over and the camera turned off was Pink. He was grinning and giving me a thumbs-up victory sign. "You were wonderful," he shouted over all the noisy conversation that had started up again.

"Thanks," I said as Mom rushed up and gave me a hug.

I waved to Mrs. Ellison as she left with Ashley a few minutes later and found my coat. The camera crew began taking down the lights and packing things up, and Marge Whitworth was barking orders at them again.

It was time to leave. Even though Ashley was already gone, I didn't want to go. I couldn't explain why. I just didn't want to, but Mom and Pink were motioning me toward the conference room door.

Officer Martin was waiting there. "I'm so glad things went so well," she said, clasping my hand warmly.

"Maybe we can set up another visit with Ashley for you sometime soon."

I thanked her and started out the door. Then I stopped. For some reason, I knew I had to look at Taffy Sinclair one more time. I turned around slowly, and she was looking at me, too. She had the same expression— sort of smiling, sort of glowing—that she had gotten on her face during the interview when I had started talking about how it felt when we found Ashley. I could tell that she was just as glad as I was that I hadn't said any more about it on television. It was too private, and it was just between Taffy and me.

12 ✱

Mom let me have a slumber party for my four best friends that night so we could all be together to watch Taffy and me on the eleven o'clock news. I was more nervous than I had been at the police station when we taped the interview.

We made a ton of popcorn and spread our sleeping bags around the living room floor as we began the long countdown to eleven o'clock.

"Aren't you just going to DIE when you see yourself on TV?" Beth shrieked. She fell backward across her sleeping bag, closed her eyes, and let her tongue loll out of one side of her mouth to imitate me dying.

"Probably," I conceded, feeling excitement rising inside me. "If I live THAT long."

Mom stuck her head in from the kitchen, where she and Pink were playing Hearts at the table. "Don't forget to call us when Marge Whitworth's show comes on."

"Don't worry, Mom. We won't forget."

Suddenly Melanie's eyes got wide with concern. "Jana, did you call Randy and remind him to watch tonight?"

"Are you kidding?" I asked, turning absolutely crimson at the idea. "I'd be too embarrassed. He knows about it. He'll probably see it anyway."

"Don't be silly," said Christie. "You shouldn't be embarrassed about calling him. Girls call boys all the time. And what about reminding Curtis? He would probably write it up for the *Mark Twain Sentinel*."

Suddenly my friends were making a list of all the kids in our class who would want to see Taffy and me on TV but might forget. Alexis Duvall and Lisa Snow and Scott Daly and Mark Peters and Kim Baxter and Sara Sawyer and even Mona Vaughn.

"What time is it?" Katie demanded.

I looked at my watch. "Five after ten."

"Super. We've got just enough time," said Katie. "Okay, Jana, since you're chicken, you get us some sodas, and the rest of us will get on the phone."

"Yeah!" said Beth. "You're going to be a STAR!"

I cringed and went slinking off to the kitchen. If they were going to do a thing like that, I was glad I didn't have to listen. I made as much noise as I could rattling ice cubes and popping the tops on soda cans, but I could still hear them in the other room laughing and talking over the phone.

Suddenly I thought of a call that I really wished I could make. To my father. I hadn't heard a word from him since I sent him the clipping from the *Bridgeport Post*. That wasn't unusual. He almost never wrote to me, but I couldn't help wishing that Marge Whitworth's show wasn't seen just in the local area, so that he could watch, too.

Just then Melanie called my name. "Okay, you can come back in now. We're finished. And don't forget to bring the sodas. Talking on the phone makes me thirsty."

I grabbed the tray of plastic glasses filled with ice and soda and went back into the living room. "Did you talk to Randy?" I asked anxiously.

"Yep," said Christie. "And all the others, too. The only one who wasn't home was Mark Peters, but we told his older brother to watch."

I passed out the sodas and sat back down on my sleeping bag. Then I looked at my watch again. It was ten minutes to eleven. Ten minutes to zero hour. I wondered if my life would pass before me like a condemned prisoner about to die when I saw myself on television. Suddenly a chill came over me. I felt cold. My legs felt cold. I glanced down. I had spilled soda and ice cubes all over my lap.

Finally it was time for the news. I switched on the set and settled back to watch as Marge Whitworth's smiling face appeared on the screen.

"Oh, Jana," squealed Melanie. "Aren't you excited?"

I nodded and glued my eyes to the TV set. "Local news making headlines tonight . . ." Miss Whitworth began. Then she went on to talk about a broken water main that flooded an underpass of the Connecticut Turnpike, a house fire where everyone got out safely, and a battle that was shaping up in the city council. Then it was time for national news.

"Why doesn't she hurry up?" demanded Katie.

I opened my mouth to explain that our interview wouldn't be part of the regular newscast since it was human interest instead of news, but before I could get anything out, Mom came racing into the room.

"Jana. Marge Whitworth is on. You forgot to call us."

Mom and Pink settled onto the sofa while the sports news came on and the weather. My friends and I were fidgeting around and exchanging impatient looks, but finally, at twenty-five past eleven, Marge Whitworth reappeared and spoke the words we had been waiting to hear.

"Ladies and gentlemen, tonight it is my privilege to present two sixth-graders from Mark Twain Elementary School here in Bridgeport and baby Ashley, the little girl they found abandoned on the school steps last Tuesday morning."

My heart jumped into my throat as the camera swung around to Taffy and me and Ashley on the table between us.

"There you are! There you are!" Beth shouted.

Little prickles danced up and down my spine as I looked myself over. My hair looked great, and Mom had been right about my pale blue sweater with the lace collar being perfect for TV. Then I checked out Taffy Sinclair. Of course, she looked gorgeous. By now Miss Whitworth was introducing me. My face turned red, but deep down I was terribly proud.

Nobody said anything else until the interview was over. I held my breath that none of my friends would notice the look that passed between Taffy and me. No one did. They were all too busy telling me how wonderful I was and going on and on about how darling Ashley looked.

"You know what I wonder?" Katie asked a little while later, after we had turned off the television set and snuggled down into our sleeping bags to go to sleep.

"What?" I asked. I was feeling drowsy, and I hoped Katie wasn't going to start on some big lecture the way she did sometimes.

"I wonder if Ashley's mother was watching."

She said the words quietly, but they echoed in my brain as loud as thunder. I frowned. "So what?" I challenged.

"I just can't help wondering what she was thinking," said Katie.

"I'll bet she was glad to see that Ashley is okay," offered Melanie.

"Why would she be?" I grumbled. "She's the one who abandoned her. That's just the same as throwing her away."

"No, it isn't," argued Christie. "My mother and I were talking about it last night. There are a lot worse things she could have done instead of leaving her on the school steps."

"And she was bundled up all warm in her basket," added Beth. "And her mother had left a bottle in there in case she got hungry."

"Don't forget the note," said Melanie. "It was a nice note. It told her name and said 'Please take good care of me.' I don't think a mean mother would have left a note like that."

I wanted to say that I did, but I kept my mouth shut. How could they have sympathy for anyone who would leave such a precious baby as Ashley alone out in the cold? They didn't understand how it had felt to find her. Only Taffy Sinclair and I understood that.

Still, as I lay there in the dark, I couldn't help wondering about Ashley's mother, too. What was she like? Was she young or old, and what did she look like? I closed my eyes and tried to picture her, but I couldn't. A million other questions jumbled around in my mind, also. Did she know that the police were looking for her? Did she feel like a criminal? Was she scared? Was she sorry now that she had abandoned her baby?

But the biggest question of all was, how could a person abandon someone they loved? I thought about my father and how I had seen some similarities in Ashley's situation and mine. I had thought that, in a way, my father had abandoned me, too. So did my father really love me? And did Ashley's mother love her?

My friends had all drifted off to sleep, and Beth was even snoring a funny little *ka-poof, ka-poof* sound. I wanted to go to sleep, too, but I couldn't. I wasn't the least bit sleepy anymore. Ashley's mother was on my mind. Maybe if I could figure out how she felt about Ashley, I could understand how my father felt about me.

13 *

The next morning my friends and I had a big pancake
breakfast, which we made ourselves after we promised
Mom we would clean everything up. It was great, and I
was stuffed. At breakfast nobody mentioned Ashley's
mother again. Mostly they talked about how great I
looked on TV and about how Taffy Sinclair bragged
about being in a soap opera. And of course they talked
about Ashley.

"When are you going to see her again?" asked
Melanie.

"I don't know. Maybe next Saturday. Mom has to call
the police station and see if it's okay."

Melanie bit her lower lip as if she was trying to get up her nerve to say something else. "Do you think we could go with you if you asked the police really nice?"

"Oh, yes!" shouted Beth. "Do it, Jana. Ask if we can see Ashley, too. PLEASE."

I looked around the table at my friends. I was dying to show her off to them. "Sure. I can even show you how to hold her and things like that."

After they left I went in to talk to Mom about it. She was sitting on the sofa reading the Sunday paper.

"Mom. I have a favor to ask."

"Sure, honey. What is it?"

The paper was spread all over the sofa, and as I brushed part of it aside to sit down beside her, I noticed a picture on one page that made me catch my breath. It was Ashley. I grabbed it and held it up. "Look, Mom. Here's something more about our baby."

Mom and I leaned together to look at the article, and then I began reading it out loud.

"Hundreds of offers have poured in from all over the country from families wanting to adopt the baby known only as Ashley who was abandoned on the front steps of Mark Twain Elementary School last Tuesday."

I stopped reading for a second as the idea sunk in. "Adopt Ashley?" I said just above a whisper. "I never thought about anything like that."

"Go on, Jana." Mom urged. "Read the rest of it."

I nodded.

"One of the most touching offers came from right here in Bridgeport when Mr. and Mrs. Walter Sinclair, parents of one of the sixth-grade girls who found the baby . . ."

"MOM!" I shrieked, dropping the paper as if it were a red-hot poker. "Not Taffy Sinclair! Not Taffy's parents adopting Ashley!"

"Calm down, sweetheart." Then Mom reached out and put her arm around me, pulling my head onto her shoulder. "Nobody has said that Ashley will be adopted. That will only happen if they can't find her mother or if they do find her and she is declared unfit by the court to keep her child. It's too early to know what will happen, and in the meantime, Ashley is staying with Mrs. Ellison in her foster home."

I heard all that Mom was saying, but it didn't help. Tears had started streaming down my face.

"But, Mom," I protested. "I love Ashley. I love her more than anybody does. More than Taffy Sinclair or ANYBODY, and she loves me too. I can tell."

"Of course she loves you, honey. And nobody could deny that you love her, but just because Taffy's parents have offered to adopt her doesn't mean that they're the ones who will get her. Here, sweetheart. Blow your nose."

I took the tissue she held out and blew loudly. How could she say that? I thought angrily. She knows that Taffy Sinclair is my worst enemy in the world. I would absolutely die if she got Ashley. Taffy would never let me forget it, even for a minute. And she would brag all the time and show pictures, and she would probably tell everybody that she loved Ashley more than I did.

I closed my eyes and thought about Ashley some more. She was so sweet and precious. I wanted her for *my* little sister. I could see myself taking care of her. Feeding her. Giving her a bath. Even changing her. I wouldn't mind doing that. Not for Ashley. We would have so much fun together, and I would always protect her. As she got older, I wouldn't let anyone say anything mean to her, and I would always hold her hand when we crossed the street. Ashley and I would be sisters. It would be perfect.

Then suddenly I got this great idea. "Mom," I begged, falling down on my knees and pleading with my eyes. "Say yes. Oh, please, PLEASE say yes."

Mom got a puzzled look on her face. "Say yes about what?"

"About adopting Ashley. Call the police station. Tell them we want to adopt Ashley. Tell them we love her more than anyone and that we'll take good care of her. And, Mom," I added hastily, before she had time to say anything. "She won't be any trouble because I'll do everything for her. And she won't cost much. She's so little. She eats hardly anything. And I'll get a job to help. I'll baby-sit or something if we need extra money. Please, Mom. Oh, PLEASE!"

Mom sighed deeply and closed her eyes, leaning her head against the back of the sofa. I knew that sigh. It usually meant bad news. Mom couldn't say no. *I couldn't stand it if she said no.* If she said no, then Taffy Sinclair's parents might get to adopt Ashley.

I had to stall for time. "Mom, I've got an idea." I was trying to sound calm, but my insides were shaking like crazy. She opened her eyes and looked at me. "Think about it. Don't say no until you've had plenty of time to think it over. Take an hour." I looked quickly at my watch. "It's ten after eleven. Take until ten after twelve. Take until twelve-thirty! Then we'll talk about it again. Okay?"

She nodded. "Okay, Jana. I'll think about it until twelve-thirty."

I was nodding, too. "Okay. Great. Then we'll talk about it again. Promise?"

"Promise."

I hurried to my room so that she could think in peace. I started to take the comics along with me so that I could read my favorite strips, then changed my mind. Mom might want to read the comics herself before twelve-thirty. I didn't want her to be upset because she couldn't find them. I wanted everything to be absolutely perfect while she was thinking over adopting Ashley. I also wanted time to make a list of all the reasons why we should adopt her, just in case Mom didn't think of all of them.

I ripped a sheet of paper out of my spiral notebook and began to list reasons:

1. Because I love her.
2. Because she loves me.

3. Because she needs us.

After I wrote those three, I sat there for a long time looking at them. They were the only ones I could think of, but still, they were the most important reasons of all.

I thought twelve-thirty would never come. When it finally did, I folded the list and stuffed it into my jeans pocket. Then I opened my bedroom door a crack and peered out into the living room. Mom was still sitting on the sofa, so I tiptoed out so that I wouldn't disturb her if she was still thinking.

She looked up at me and smiled. "You're right on time." Then she patted a spot on the sofa and said, "Sit down so that we can talk."

"Did you think?" I hadn't really wanted to start our conversation that way, but the words just came bursting out before I could stop them.

"Yes, I did," said Mom. "Did you?"

"Sure. I even made a list of all the reasons we should adopt her."

"Great. That sounds like a good place to start our discussion. May I see it?"

I pulled the list out of my pocket and handed it to her. Mom smiled softly as she read them.

"These are wonderful reasons," she said. "If Ashley is put up for adoption, she certainly will need someone. Someone who will love her as much as you do. She'll need a lot of other things, too, like a good home."

"We've got that," I interjected.

"And a mother and a father," she said slowly.

"But Mom," I started to protest. "A mother and a father?" I asked, not wanting it to be true. Deep down I knew it was. "But you're a super mother," I went on. "Doesn't that count for anything?"

"Of course it does, sweetheart. It counts for a lot. But if there are other families wanting her who are super, too, and have both a mother and a father, we wouldn't stand much of a chance, would we? You've got to realize that the court will look for the best possible family for her."

I sank back against the sofa feeling as if someone were squeezing my heart. "But I LOVE her!" I insisted. Then a wonderful idea occurred to me. "Mom!" I shouted. "You and Pink are going to get married, aren't you? That would mean our family has a mother and a father. And you saw how Pink acted when he saw Ashley at the police station. He loved her, too. I know he did. He would make a wonderful father, and if you got married right away, we could still adopt Ashley. Don't you see? Oh, please!"

The smile disappeared from Mom's face. "You haven't been very enthusiastic about Pink and me getting married until now. In fact, I've had the distinct feeling lately that you didn't like the idea at all anymore."

"It would be okay," I insisted. "It really would. Then you would have Pink and I would . . ." My voice trailed off. I hadn't meant to say it that way.

"You would have Ashley," Mom said, finishing my sentence. "Is that what has been bothering you about Pink and me getting married? That we would have each other and you wouldn't have anyone?"

I buried my head in her arms. I didn't want to talk about that part of it. I only wanted to talk about Ashley.

"Jana, no matter whether Pink and I get married or not, you and I will always have each other. I promise you that. Now let's take a little more time making some of these decisions. Pink and I have plenty of time to get married, and they aren't going to allow Ashley to be adopted as long as there is a chance they can find her mother. No one is sure yet why she abandoned Ashley. Maybe she needs help."

"But, Mom," I said helplessly.

"Let me see your list again."

Reluctantly I handed it to her. I couldn't see what difference it could make.

"Look at what number one says," she said. "It's the most important."

I didn't have to look. I knew it by heart.

"It says you love her. And do you know the only way to prove how much you love someone?"

I shook my head.

"By forgetting about yourself and what will make you happy and doing something unselfish—just for her."

I grabbed my list and raced back to my room, slamming the door behind me. I had to be alone. Mom didn't understand at all. I *did* want to do something for Ashley. I wanted to be her sister and love her forever. But who was going to get to do that? Probably Taffy Sinclair.

14 ✳

*T*hat night I lay awake for a long time, staring at the ceiling. I couldn't remember when I had been more confused. Taffy Sinclair, the person I have hated all my life, was with me when we found baby Ashley, and for an instant we had almost been friends. But then, most of the time at least, we had gone back to being enemies. She tried to take all the credit for finding Ashley, and now she and her family were trying to adopt her and take her away from me.

And then there was Mom. She had been dating Pink for ages and saying that *someday* they would get married, but not right away because she didn't want to rush into anything. Suddenly, she decided to marry him without consulting me or considering my feelings. And now, when I wanted them to get married in a hurry so that our family would have a father and we could adopt Ashley instead of the Sinclairs, Mom says she wants to postpone any decisions. "*Eeeeek!!!*" I squealed. "I think I'm going bonkers."

I also couldn't forget what Mom said about my proving my love for Ashley by doing something just for her. What did she think I was doing when I asked to adopt her? Maybe I wasn't the one going bonkers, I thought. Maybe it was Mom.

I tossed and turned, unable to get Mom's words out of my mind. I tried to figure out what might make a tiny baby happy. If I were going to do something just for her, it would have to be something she would really want. Her bottle. Dry diapers. *Me for a sister.* I pushed that idea out of my mind. I knew it wasn't what Mom had meant.

What else would she want? Toys to play with. I thought about the teddy bear Taffy had brought Ashley the day of the television interview. Had Taffy been trying to prove to Ashley how much she loved her? Well, I loved her more. I just knew I did, and I would bring her a stuffed toy, only it would be twice as big as that stupid teddy bear. That would show Ashley and Taffy and Mom. It would show the whole world who loved her the most.

I crept out of bed and switched on my desk lamp. Mom had given me my allowance yesterday, and I hadn't spent any of it. Plus I had a little saved up. I knew

I didn't possibly have enough to buy a big toy for Ashley, but I counted it anyway. "Oh, brother," I whispered to myself. "Only seven dollars and twenty-five cents. I can't even buy a *little* toy for that."

I turned out the light and crawled back into bed, trying to think of something else a baby would want. Babies were so little, and there wasn't much they could do. How could they really want anything?

On the way to school the next morning I was so deep in thought, still trying to figure out what to do for Ashley, that I didn't hear Randy Kirwan come up behind me.

"Hey, Jana. I saw you on TV Saturday night," he said.

I almost jumped out of my skin. Then I blushed when I saw that he was giving me his 1,000-watt smile. I didn't know what to say, so I just smiled back.

"I'll bet it was pretty exciting."

I nodded, "It was, and scary, too."

"You looked really nice," he said, and I blushed again. "Especially your hair. Which was the most exciting? Being on television or finding Ashley?"

"Finding Ashley." I didn't even have to think about that. "She's the most beautiful baby in the whole world, and I really love her."

Randy fell into step with me, and we walked along in silence for a moment. I was thinking about what a kind and sensitive person he is and how some day he would make a wonderful father.

"Do you know anything about babies?" I saw the quizzical look on his face and added quickly, "You know. What they want and what they like best and things like that?"

Randy shrugged. "The usual stuff, I guess. Their bottles and dry diapers." He paused and then he gave a funny little laugh. "And their mothers. My little cousin, Matthew, throws a pure fit when my aunt Chris even leaves the room."

I sighed. Randy was no help, either. When we adopted Ashley, Mom would be her mother, and I would be with her always. I would never leave the room if she didn't want me to. But that wasn't going to help me now.

Randy's voice broke into my thoughts again. "What's going on at school?" He was pointing to a crowd of kids, mostly sixth-graders, clustered near the swings.

"Come on," I said. "Let's go find out."

We trotted across the street and onto the school ground. Just then someone walked away from the crowd, leaving a gap big enough for me to see who it was that was the center of attention. I should have known. It was Taffy Sinclair.

I wanted to turn around, but Randy was still heading toward the crowd, so I kept going. She's probably bragging about being on television, I thought with disgust. I could just hear her telling everyone what a big star she was and how she would probably have her own show any day now. But to my surprise, that wasn't what she was saying, at all. It was worse.

". . . and the people at the police station said they thought we would have a VERY good chance of getting to adopt Ashley. Isn't that super? It's the most exciting thing that has ever happened to me in my whole life!"

I shot a quick sideways glance at Randy. He was staring straight at Taffy and he looked impressed. I thought I'd die.

Just then my four best friends came walking up, and I took them aside and filled them in on what was going on. "It's the most disgusting thing in the world," I said.

Beth nodded. "I read about it in yesterday's paper. What are you going to do?"

"Are you going to try to adopt her, too?" Melanie asked.

"Mom said we wouldn't stand a chance because they will want her to have a family with a FATHER. I don't see what difference that makes. Mom and I have been alone without a father for ages, and we get along just fine." Then I went on to tell them what Mom had said about the real way to prove that you love someone. "What am I going to do?" I pleaded. "I've just got to prove to Ashley and everybody that I love that baby more than Taffy Sinclair and her parents do. That's the only way Mom and I will stand a chance to adopt her."

My friends all looked at me sympathetically. Christie shook her head. "I don't know, Jana. That's tough."

"It sure is," added Katie.

They were no help. I thought and thought all day long. I almost got into trouble once in social studies class for not paying attention. Wiggins called on me, and I didn't even hear the question, much less know the answer.

After school, Taffy Sinclair just happened to stop by my locker. I tried to ignore her, but she stood there with that icky sweet smile on her face until I thought I would explode.

"What do you want?"

"I just wondered if you had heard the news about how my parents will probably adopt Ashley and she'll be MY little sister."

I snickered. "No, she won't. Not if Mom and I have anything to say about it."

I slammed my locker door and got out of there, leaving her standing alone, smiling her icky sweet smile at the back of my head. All I wanted to do was get home and talk to Mom.

❀ ❀ ❀

I threw my books on the sofa and went into the kitchen to fix myself a snack. Mom wouldn't be home for half an hour. I still hadn't solved the problem of what to do for Ashley to prove I loved her. I smiled when I remembered asking Randy what babies like. As if a boy would know, I thought. *The usual stuff, I guess*, he had said. *Their bottles and dry diapers. And their mothers. My little cousin, Matthew, throws a pure fit when my aunt Chris even leaves the room.* AND THEIR MOTHERS. Why hadn't I thought of that?

Of course, that was it. What Ashley probably wanted most of all was her mother. In some ways it was the same as my wanting my father all these years. Or even if Ashley didn't want her mother as much as I thought she did, there was only one way to know for sure. I had to find her. That was the only way I would ever know if she had hurt Ashley or why she had abandoned her. And if she really loved her. I had to know that or it would worry me the rest of my life. But most of all, I had to do it for Ashley.

Just then I realized that I was still standing in the middle of the kitchen, but I hadn't fixed myself a snack. I hadn't even opened the refrigerator door. I didn't want a snack. I wasn't the least bit hungry anymore. I had an idea. It was a way to find Ashley's mother that just might work. I smiled to myself. But to do it, I needed my mother.

15 ✱

*M*om sighed when I told her my plan, and I could tell that she didn't hold out much hope for its working. But she said, yes, she would put a classified advertisement in the *Bridgeport Post* for me. After all, she *is* the classified ad manager in charge of all the ads that go into the paper.

"I'll write it myself," I said. "In fact, I've already been working on it. How does this sound?

"*Dear Baby Ashley's Mother: You probably know that Ashley is okay. That's been on TV. But do you know how much she misses you? I can tell you all about it if you want to call me. My name is Jana, and I'm one of the girls who found her. My number is five five five, oh two five oh.*"

"That's beautiful, Jana. I'll put it in tomorrow's paper in the personals column and let it run for three days. How's that?"

"Super." Three whole days, I thought happily. Surely Ashley's mother would see it in that time.

"I'll pay for it with my own money," I offered. "I have seven dollars and twenty-five cents. If that's not enough, I'll take the rest out of my next allowance."

"Sure, honey. You won't be billed for a few days anyway. We'll work it out then." She paused, and her expression got serious. "I don't want to upset you, but I hope you won't be too disappointed if you don't hear from her."

I started to answer, but she held up her hand. "Ashley's mother may have left Bridgeport right after she abandoned her baby. The authorities don't think Ashley was born here, so maybe her mother was just passing through. And even if she is here, there's no guarantee that she'll read your ad or call you if she does." Then Mom took both my hands in hers and said in a very soft voice, "I think what you're doing is wonderful, Jana. It's sweet and unselfish. It certainly proves how much you really do love Ashley. I just don't want you to be hurt if it doesn't work out."

I nodded. I was afraid I would cry if I said anything. Ashley's mother had to read my ad. She just *had* to. That's all there was to it. Besides, Mom was always bragging about how many people read the *Bridgeport*

Post classified ads and what good results the people who placed them always got. It would work out for me. I knew it would.

The next day was Tuesday. It was not only the day that my ad would be in the paper, but it was also the one-week anniversary of our finding Ashley. I couldn't believe that it had only been a week. It seemed as if that baby had been a part of my life forever. At school, everybody had pretty much forgotten about Ashley, and so Taffy and I weren't celebrities anymore. In fact, Clarence Marshall was getting most of the attention. His father had had a spectacular one-car accident on the Merritt Parkway and walked away without a scratch, and Clarence was telling anyone who would listen all the details, complete with sound effects.

I raced home after school to wait for Mom to get there with the paper. I hadn't told anyone about it. Not even my best friends. I can't exactly explain why I kept it a secret. It was just too private, I guess. I slipped into the apartment and went straight to my room. I had planned to do my homework early so that I could sit by the phone all evening. I also needed time to rehearse what I would say when Ashley's mother called. I went over some possibilities in my mind.

Hello, Jana. This is Ashley's mother, a voice would say. It would be a nice voice. Full of kindness and love. *I'm so glad that someone like you found her. I know you'll always take good care of her. Good-bye.*

At first I felt really good about that voice, but then my feeling of contentment faded. If Ashley's mother turned out to be that nice, why did she abandon her baby in the first place?

Then I heard another voice. *I'm glad you have that little brat*, it said angrily. *She did nothing but cry and wet her pants.* I slammed down the phone in my imagination. I couldn't talk to someone like that. Besides, it hurt too much to think that Ashley's mother might be that kind of person.

I decided to get my homework done and out of the way, and I was almost finished when Mom got home.

"Jana," she called from the living room. "I have the paper."

I dashed to meet her and took the paper out of her hand. She already had it opened to the page where my ad appeared and had circled it in red. I read it through at least six times. She had put it in exactly the way I wrote it. Now all I had to do was wait for the phone to ring.

Mom made meat loaf for supper, and even though it's one of my favorites, I couldn't eat. I mostly just pushed it around my plate. Mom didn't say anything. I guess she knew that my mind was on other things.

I kept imagining Ashley's mother was picking up the paper at that very moment. I could almost see her as she opened it to the classified ads. She would look casually down the page and then stop as the word "Ashley" would practically jump out at her. She would read the ad, and slowly a smile would spread across her face. She would gaze off into the distance for a moment as if she were seeing her baby again. Then she would race to the phone and punch in the number in the ad. I looked sharply at the phone. I knew that any second it was going to ring. But it didn't.

It didn't ring while I was drying dishes for Mom, either. Once, a little while later, I even double-checked the ad to make sure they had gotten the telephone number right.

Later, something else began to worry me. What if our phone was out of order? It hadn't rung all evening. Maybe the line was dead or something like that? If I picked it up and listened and there was a dial tone, I would know that it was not out of order. But if I picked it up and listened at the wrong moment, I could miss the call from Ashley's mother. Of course, if she got a busy signal, she could always call back later. But what if she didn't? What if she chickened out? Or changed her mind? Or lost her quarter for the pay phone? A million things could happen to keep her from calling back. I didn't dare pick up that receiver, no matter how much I wanted to. It could be a terrible mistake.

I tried to watch television with Mom, but I didn't even know what shows were on. Mom kept trying to cheer me up. "Why don't we make some popcorn?" she suggested. Normally I would volunteer to jump through fiery hoops for popcorn, or stand on my head while juggling teacups with my feet, but not tonight. "No, thanks," I said. "I'm still not hungry."

Mom allowed me to stay up an hour past my bedtime, and then she promised that she would wake me if anyone called. I crawled into bed, feeling awfully depressed. I had been so sure that Ashley's mother would call by now.

Mom stuck her head in the door to tell me good-night. "There's always tomorrow," she said. "Some people don't have time to read the evening paper until the next day. Don't give up, sweetheart. It's too early for that."

I couldn't stand keeping my ad a secret anymore, so I tore it out of the paper, and as soon as I got to school the next morning, I showed it to my friends.

"Gosh, Jana," said Katie. "That's a great idea."

"I think so, too," said Christie. "My parents sold our old car through the classified ads. We had forty-seven calls. I think just about everybody reads the ads in the *Post*."

"I don't know," said Beth, shaking her head. "Why would Ashley's mother be reading them in the first place? There's no reason for her to think that anyone would put in an ad about Ashley. Sorry, Jana. I really don't think it will work."

"It will, TOO," I protested. "Who knows? Maybe she'll want to buy a car or something, and she'll just happen to look in the personals column and see my ad. I know she'll call. Just wait and see."

That night I started my vigil by the telephone again. It did seem a little strange that nobody at school had mentioned seeing my ad. Surely some of their parents read the classifieds. Still, I wasn't going to let what Beth said discourage me. She didn't *always* know what she was talking about.

By eight o'clock I was really getting antsy. If Ashley's mother didn't call pretty soon, I knew I'd die. Just then the phone rang. I jumped so high you would have thought I was on a trampoline.

"It's the phone, Jana. Aren't you going to get it?" Mom asked in an excited voice.

"Sure," I mumbled and picked up the receiver. This was probably it. The call I had been waiting for. My voice was shaking as I said hello.

"Hi, Jana. It's Melanie. Has Ashley's mother called yet?"

"What!?" I shrieked. "Melanie! Get off the phone! She could be trying to call right this minute."

"Sor-RY!" Melanie huffed and slammed down the receiver. I knew I had been rude, but what did she think she was doing calling at such an important time?

I was too nervous to sit still after that. Melanie's call could have spoiled everything. I started pacing the floor, stopping once in a while to look out the window and watch the traffic go by. I could tell that I was making Mom almost as nervous as I was, but I couldn't help it.

Then the phone rang again. "You get it this time, Mom," I whispered. I held my breath as she picked up the receiver.

"Hello?" Then she shot me an apologetic look. "Oh, hi, Pink. No. No one has called, and we're trying to keep the line open. Talk to you tomorrow. Bye."

"What's the matter with everybody?" I cried. Then I realized what I had said. "Sorry, Mom. It's just that everyone knows how important this is."

"That's right, honey. Nobody means to cause you any problems. They just care about you. That's why they can't resist calling to see if you've had any luck yet. Why don't you get ready for bed now? You look exhausted. I'll wake you if your call comes through."

The instant she said that, I realized how tired I was. I nodded and went to my room, changing into my pajamas. I scuffed into the bathroom and turned on the water. I wanted to brush my teeth as fast as I could before I fell asleep standing at the sink. My mouth was full of foamy toothpaste when I heard the phone ring again. I dropped the brush in the sink and burst out the door. Mom had answered it, and she had a strange look on her face.

"Yes, Officer Martin. What is it?"

My heart stopped. Officer Martin? What was wrong?

"Oh, dear," Mom said. "Yes, I understand. Is she okay?"

It had to be Ashley! She was hurt! The awful person who had abused her had found her again! I ran to Mom, grabbing her arm and pleading with my eyes.

"Certainly, Officer Martin. We'll be right there."
Then Mom turned to me and said, "It's Ashley's
mother, sweetheart. They've found her. She's in the
hospital, and she's asking for you."

16 *

*O*fficer Martin was waiting for us just inside the emergency room door when our taxi pulled up in front of the hospital. There was only one other person in the waiting room, a man with a towel wrapped around one hand.

The police officer greeted us warmly and motioned us to some chairs in a corner. "Thanks for coming. Let's go over here where we can talk before I take you in to see Mrs. Adamson."

Mrs. Adamson? I thought. That must be Ashley's mother. Ashley Adamson. I hadn't thought about her having a last name before.

"Let me begin by telling you a little bit about Ashley's mother," said Officer Martin. "She is in serious condition from a beating." The police officer paused and looked at me sadly. "Ashley's father is the one who beat her, Jana. He beat her up a lot of times. She's what we commonly call a battered wife."

"Poor Mrs. Adamson," I whispered. I had heard about battered wives before. Suddenly I felt very sorry for her. Maybe she wasn't the terrible person I had imagined she was, after all.

"When they brought her into the emergency room, she was only partly conscious and she was trying to say something. But no one could understand her. She had a scrap of paper in her hand. She wouldn't let anyone take it from her or even see what it was. Then, when she regained full consciousness, she showed it to the nurse and said she wanted to use the phone. Jana, honey, it was your ad in the personals column of the *Bridgeport Post*. If it hadn't been for that ad, she might have kept her secret forever. Then everyone here at the hospital would have thought she was just another emergency room case and would not have mentioned the ad to the police, and we would never have found Ashley's mother."

I felt Mom's arm slip around my shoulder. I leaned against her, feeling better, but there was a question I had to ask. "And what about Ashley? Did her father give her that bruise on her stomach, too?"

"Yes, I'm afraid he did. Like I said, he had beaten her mother many times, but when he turned on Ashley, she decided that she had to do something to save her little girl. She was afraid he might hurt Ashley again. But don't worry. He's been arrested. He won't be able to hurt her anymore. Would you like to see Mrs. Adamson now? She's very anxious to meet you."

I sat there, staring at Officer Martin. I wanted desperately to see Ashley's mother. I had wanted to know about her almost from the beginning. And to understand why she had abandoned her baby. But part of me *didn't* want to see her. If she were all the good things Officer Martin said, then Ashley wouldn't be put up for adoption, and Mom and I would never have the chance to love her and take care of her. I would never get to be her sister.

Officer Martin stood up. She was waiting for me to answer. I looked at Mom. She had a sympathetic look on her face. She understood what I was thinking. I knew she did. But she didn't say anything. She was waiting for me to make my own decision.

I thought about Ashley again. She was so beautiful, and I loved her so much. Still, deep down I knew that she needed her mother. That was why I had put the ad in the paper in the first place.

"Okay," I said, and I stood up, too.

When we tiptoed into Mrs. Adamson's room, I caught my breath and grabbed Mom's hand. Ashley's mother was lying in the bed with her eyes closed. Even in the dark I could see the bruises on her face.

She opened her eyes when we walked in, and when she realized who it was, she tried to smile, but I could tell that it hurt. "Hello, you must be Jana," she said in a voice just above a whisper. "I'm so glad you came."

I dropped Mom's hand and went to her bed. "Hi," I said. "How are you feeling?" The minute I said that, I felt silly. She was feeling rotten. Anyone could see that. But she didn't seem to mind my asking. She even tried to smile again.

Even though she was pretty bruised up, I couldn't help thinking how much Ashley looked like her. Mrs. Adamson had blue eyes and reddish-gold curls, just like Ashley's.

"I want to thank you for finding Ashley and taking such good care of her," she said. "You saved her life. If it hadn't been for you two girls . . ." Her voice trailed off as she began to cry. Softly at first, and then she broke into sobs.

"It's okay," I said, taking her hand and patting it. It was all I could think of to do. "Ashley's fine. And she's so beautiful. And she smiles and gurgles all the time. And I just know she's going to be glad to see you."

Officer Martin stepped forward. "I think we'd better go now and let Mrs. Adamson rest."

"Okay." I knew I should say good-night and leave, but I couldn't go just yet. There was one more thing I had to know. "Mrs. Adamson?" I said softly. "Can I ask you something?"

She nodded.

"Why did you leave Ashley at our school?"

She sighed and got a faraway look on her face. "When I was a little girl, I didn't have a happy family life, but I loved school. It was the only place where I could smile and laugh, and my teachers were so nice to me. So when I knew that I couldn't keep Ashley with me any longer, I decided to take her to a school. I knew it was a place where children were loved and cared for. And then"— she paused for a moment—"when I put her on the steps and walked out through the playground gate, I realized that the bell had already rung and that it might be hours before anyone found her. I couldn't just leave her there in the cold, so I turned around to go back and get her and try to figure out something else to do. But when I looked through the gate again, I saw a girl run out of the building and pick her up and then take her back inside, and I knew that Ashley was going to be okay."

She had been there all the time! My heart jumped into my throat. She had been standing there watching when Taffy Sinclair brought Ashley into the school. She hadn't really abandoned her. She had known all along that her baby was safe. I was so glad I thought I'd die.

I couldn't help thinking about my father just then and how Ashley and I had so many things in common. Was it possible that my father had done what he thought was best all these years by staying away from me since he's an alcoholic? Maybe he hadn't really abandoned me after all. Maybe he had left me with Mom where he knew I'd be safe.

We left right after that. Officer Martin gave us a ride back home, and on the way she told us more of the story. She said that Ashley had been born in Boston, Massachusetts, which was why the police couldn't find any record of her birth in Connecticut. Her father had lost his job and had brought the family to Bridgeport while he looked for work. And every day he bought a *Bridgeport Post* and read the help wanted column in the classified ads.

After we got back home, Mom made us some hot chocolate. "Why didn't Mrs. Adamson call the police herself when she got beaten up?" I asked as I sipped my cocoa.

"I think she was probably just too scared," said Mom. "She was afraid that even if her husband went to jail, he'd get out and hurt her again."

"But won't that happen now, anyway?"

Mom shook her head. "Officer Martin told me that they are going to turn her case over to a special agency that helps people like her. They'll help her start a new life with Ashley. Maybe even change her name. She'll be safe now."

"Do you think I'll ever get to see Ashley again?"

Mom smiled. "I hope so. In fact, I'm sure her mother will never forget you and Taffy Sinclair and what you did for her. Who knows? You both might get to see her again sooner than you think."

"Both?" I grumbled. "Taffy didn't find Ashley's mother for her. I did. Besides, she's always trying to make people think that she found Ashley by herself, and that I had nothing to do with it. I don't understand that because . . ." I paused a moment. "Mom, I've never told anyone this before, but when Taffy and I found Ashley, for a few minutes it felt like we were best friends. And now . . ."

"And now things are back to the way they used to be," Mom said. "Is that what you're trying to say?"

"I guess so," I admitted. "Except that every once in a while we get that good feeling back again."

Mom nodded. "That happens to people sometimes when they've shared a special experience. Like being stranded together in a blizzard, for instance . . . or finding an abandoned baby," she added softly. "It brought out the very best in both of you. Don't be disappointed that the feeling couldn't last. It was too intense. But I can promise you one thing, neither one of you will *ever* forget it."

I nodded happily and told her good-night. I climbed in bed, thinking that in the morning I would have to wake up early and call Taffy. I wanted to tell her myself about Ashley's mother and all the things that had happened tonight before Officer Martin or someone else told her. I hoped that she would be as glad as I was that everything was working out okay for our baby. Deep down, I knew she would. She loved Ashley, too.

I also knew that Mom was right. We would probably always be enemies. But still, as I snuggled into my pillow and drifted off to sleep, I knew that every time Taffy Sinclair or I saw a little baby, we would think about each other and how special it had felt when we found baby Ashley—together.

ABOUT THE AUTHOR

BETSY HAYNES, the daughter of a former news-woman, began scribbling poetry and short stories as soon as she learned to write. A serious writing career, however, had to wait until after her marriage and the arrival of her two children. But that early practice must have paid off, for within three months Mrs. Haynes had sold her first story. In addition to a number of magazine short stories, *The Great Mom Swap*, *The Great Boyfriend Trap*, and the Taffy Sinclair series, Mrs. Haynes is the author of The Fabulous Five series, which features the five best friends from the Taffy Sinclair books. She lives in Colleyville, Texas, with her husband, who is the author of a young adult novel.

☐ **THE SARA SUMMER** 15600/$2.75
by Mary Downing Hahn
Twelve-year-old Emily Sherwood has grown like a beanstalk and all the kids are calling her "Giraffe." What's worse, her best friend has deserted her. Things seem pretty bad until Sara, a tall, tough, wacky and wise New Yorker teaches Emily a thing or two about life.

☐ **YOU'RE GOING OUT THERE A** 15577/$2.50
KID, BUT YOU'RE COMING BACK A STAR
by Linda Hirsch
Margaret Dapple is ten years old and tired of waiting around to grow up, tired of waiting for everyone—especially her parents and big sister Barbara—to recognize that she is not a baby anymore. So Margaret decides to show them all—she's going to improve her image.

☐ **NOW IS NOT TOO LATE** 15548/$2.75
by Isabelle Holland
When Cathy arrives on the island to spend the summer with her grandmother, her summer friends warn her to stay away from the Wicked Witch, who turns out to be hauntingly familiar and not a witch at all.

☐ **THE SISTERS IMPOSSIBLE** 26013/$2.50
by J. D. Landis
As sisters go, Saundra and Lily have never been the best of friends. But the real trouble starts when their father buys younger sister Lily a pair of dancing shoes so she can go to ballet school with the beautiful and accomplished Saundra.

☐ **ANASTASIA KRUPNIK** 15534/$2.75
by Lois Lowry
To Anastasia Krupnik, being ten is very confusing. On top of everything her parents are going to have a baby—at their age! It's enough to make a kid want to do something terrible . . .